The Cage

First Book of The Birthright Series

by

Jacci Turner

The Cage
First Book in The Birthright Series
Copyright 2011, Jacci Turner
Cover by Chris Heifner

Published by
Lucky Bat Books
LuckyBatBooks.com

DEDICATION

To David. My lover, best friend and biggest fan. I couldn't have done it without you!

TABLE OF CONTENTS

CHAPTER ONE
RUDE AWAKENINGS

S AM BROWN LEANED HER BIRD-LIKE frame against the building wall, trying to get warm in a sliver of morning sunlight. Gripping her sketch pad as blood-red ink dried around her freshly finished poem. Sam's eyes were glued to the front door of a portable classroom down the hill from where she stood. There, she would spend the next four weeks repeating English 102.

A low roar caught her attention as a tall, brown-haired man rounded the corner of the portable classroom on a skateboard. No, it was not a normal skateboard; it was longer, the kind kids used to travel distances. Sam was shocked when she realized how old he looked. What was he, thirty? Who did this guy think he was? Some kind of wannabe teenager? Then, to her surprise, he jumped off the longboard and headed up the steps to the portable classroom, unlocking the door with a key from a jingling chain. This idiot was her teacher? This was ridiculous. How was she supposed to learn anything from a guy who rode a longboard to class? Sam had only been at McQueen High School for one semester, but had certainly never seen a teacher this young before, and never one riding a longboard.

Sam wondered what her teacher would think of her if he could see her. She tried to see herself from his perspective, a small creature in black clothes. Hair dyed jet black, falling across a pale face. Skin cloaked in a thick, severe mask of makeup. He'd see her as a freak. Everyone saw her that way.

It didn't matter to her, she just had to retake this stupid class, get a better grade, and get out. She could put up with a lame teacher for four weeks. After all, she had put up with worse. Glancing down, her eyes scanned the new poem silently.

Closing The Cage Door

The cage door slammed shut when I was young.

The monster cat trapped me inside,

smacking his lips in anticipation of the kill.

This bird would fly no more,

Wings were not the only things clipped that day.

Dreams, hopes and heart were also ripped away.

No one heard the cries, or thought to listen.

Only one lesson was learned

Only one is still needed.

No one cares.

Sam stood watching as students started filing into the classroom below. Finally, when she could wait no longer, she trudged down the hill to yet another kind of cage.

Tyrell jerked bolt upright in bed, his sheets damp with sweat. His heart pounded as he tried to get his bearings. This was in his bedroom. He was not chasing the blonde through the truck-stop parking lot.

"Stupid, stupid dream!"

Kicking off his tangled sheets, he swung his feet onto the floor of the dark room. Running his thumb across his phone, he checked the time, three-thirty A.M.

"Damn."

Of the whole summer vacation this was the one night he'd wanted to sleep and he'd been awakened by that stupid dream again. Why couldn't that blonde girl just leave him alone? What did she want with him, anyway?

The dream had started a few months ago. It was always the same. He was chasing a blonde girl through a truck-stop parking lot. She needed help and he was supposed to help her, but he didn't know why or how. The dream was becoming more real each time he had it. Now it was intense enough to wake him up in the middle of the night.

Lying back on his bed, he tried to relax enough to go back to sleep, but his mind raced. Today was the first day of summer school English class. He hated to admit he was nervous about it. Why didn't they have summer school at his own school this year? Proctor Hug High School was where most of Reno's African American kids went. He felt comfortable there. But because of budget cuts this year they were only having summer school at a few sites. He had to go to Mc-Queen. McQueen High School was over in old northwest Reno and was known as the Academy on the Hill, or as McQueer, depending on who was talking. He smiled at the thought. Of course, Hug was known as "Thug" too.

Tyrell disregarded this; he liked his school. He had friends there and knew his place there. He wondered what it would be like to be around a bunch of spoiled white kids all summer. None of his friends were taking summer school, but then none of his friends were as particular about their grades.

Summer school was a stupid idea. Tyrell rolled over, trying to relax, so he could sleep a few more hours before his alarm went off.

TIFFANY SAT IN THE BACK of her mom's car, slouching against the door frame. Her brother, Hanju, was slumped against the driver's passenger side door pretending to be asleep. She didn't know what was worse, having to get up early for summer school, or going in and working at the dry cleaners all day like Hanju. Her mother's voice, like a bee buzzing around her, continued to lecture Tiffany about doing well in summer school. She wondered if her mother had taken one breath since she'd left home. She'd tuned her out a long time ago but threw out an obedient "Yes Uma" occasionally so her mom would think she was still listening.

Why should she listen? Hadn't she memorized this lecture? Her parents had sacrificed everything, leaving good jobs in Korea to come to America and give their children a better life. What ungrateful children they were not to appreciate their parents suffering, blah blah blah blah. She was sick of it.

Tiffany knew her mother couldn't see her, even if she glanced back in the review mirror she would see Tiffany's body, but not who she really was. *She has never seen me. She has no idea what I like or dislike, what I want for my life, or what is important to me.* Of course, if her mother *had* really known what she wanted, she would be devastated. Tiffany wanted freedom! She wanted to be her own person, independent, like the girls at her school. She wanted to speak what was on her mind, and not constantly run everything though the grid of her guilt-soaked brain.

Suddenly, she knew exactly what she would do. She would be at a new school where she knew no one. A new school with no familiar faces would allow her to be anyone she wanted to be. *Today, I am going to say whatever comes to my mind. Today, I am going to be free, and honest and independent.* A slight nod of her head was the only sign of her new resolution, and her mother would think it was just another sign of agreement.

ORLANDO'S BED WAS SHAKING. Was it an earthquake, he wondered? Then he heard his mother's voice. "Hijo, hurry up, you need to catch the bus or you'll be late." Orlando grunted, and turned over, seeing his mother in her bathrobe shaking his bed.

"What Ma?"

"Your class, remember? Today is the first day of your summer school class. Do you want to be late?"

Orlando sat up slowly, rubbing his eyes. He wanted to sleep; it was summer! Going to summer school had *not* been his idea and he resented it. Just how important was it to get ahead in English anyway? He started to say something mean to his mother but bit back the retort. She was waking him up after returning from her swing shift job at the casino. Had she even been to sleep yet? The fact that she and his Abuela pinned all their hopes on Orlando was not lost to him. He felt the pressure of it every day. Sometimes it was suffocating.

Swinging his legs out of bed, he slowly rose to his feet. His mother left the room and went into the kitchen to make his breakfast. He just wanted to stay home and play video games. Now he had to get up early and take the bus across town to a school he didn't even know. He was *not* happy.

CHAPTER TWO
ENGLISH 102

MR. MONAHAN WATCHED AS THE SIXTEEN students slunk into his Sophomore English classroom. He thought they looked young. They headed for chairs as far from him, and from each other, as possible. He was used to teaching Senior Advanced Placement English, and these students looked nothing like those who had just graduated. *What a difference two years makes,* he thought.

Dismayed by the warm June sun he was missing, he glanced out the window to escape the institutional grey walls of his portable classroom. Backpacking through Europe had been his plan – instead of being trapped in a hot cage.

This place probably becomes an oven during the summer.

Sharing the dream of a summer in Ireland to celebrate their marriage, he and Sarah had been crushed when the newspaper laid her off. A fourth-year teacher's salary barely paid the bills, not with the dollar's value shrinking each day. He knew he should be grateful to have a job, even if it meant having to work this summer instead of traveling out of the country.

Slowly, he became aware the room was quiet and sixteen pairs of eyes were studying him. *It's time to seize the moment. The sooner we get started, the sooner I'll be outside.*

Grabbing a stack of spiral notebooks, he began to walk from desk to desk, placing a notebook on each as he spoke.

"Welcome to Sophomore English. My name is Mr. Monahan. These will be your journals for the class. The syllabus is folded inside the front cover. Read the syllabus, people. There are extra assignments in there, so read it thoroughly!

"Please put your name on the outside of the journal immediately. You are welcome to decorate your cover with appropriate artwork if you like. No gang, violent, or pornographic images, please."

There was a small, uncertain wave of laughter from some students.

"Ah," said Mr. Monahan, "a sign of life."

He stepped up to the front of the class and leaned his tall, sturdy frame against his desk.

"You will have a journal assignment each day and you will turn your journals in to me each Friday. You will be graded on your writing as this is an English class, but your participation grade will be what matters most. Each day you will read and discuss what you have written in your journal with your group. You will grade each other on your participation. I will grade you on the progress you make in this class."

An audible groan escaped from the lips of several students. Mr. Monahan stood his full height and ran his hand backwards over curly brown hair.

"I know it seems harsh, but we only have four weeks, people, and I don't want to be stuck inside in the middle of the summer any more than you do. So, we are going to make this as interesting as possible. I want full cooperation: everybody writes, every day, no excuses. I want full par-ti-ci-pa-tion: everybody reads out-loud, every day, no excuses. I want perfect attendance. You miss once and you'd better be in the hospital. You miss twice, you flunk. Understand?"

Mr. Monahan stood still and looked at each student. He wanted to be sure they understood this part perfectly so it didn't come back on him later. "Four weeks, people, no room for error. Four days a week. You cannot miss two days and pass, got it?"

Several heads nodded in agreement.

"My classroom instruction will be based on what I observe in your journals. I will teach on the most common mistakes I see each week. I know you are here for different reasons. Some of you are taking this class before your sophomore year to get ahead in credits. Some of you are taking this class after your sophomore year because you didn't earn the credits the first time."

Again, a small ripple of laughter ran through the class.

"I'm not concerned about why you are taking the class. I'm only concerned you learn something while you are here. Show up every day and write every night, read every morning and you will get full credit for the class. It's an easy grade, right? No one should flunk this class!

"Alright, now I've broken you up into groups of four. Because you represent four different high schools, I want you to get to know each other in the next four weeks. You will be in the same group for the whole four weeks of class. You will now stand and find the three others in the room who have the same color notebook you have. When you find them, please turn your desks toward each other, and face me, so I can show you how I want you to introduce yourselves."

He leaned back against his desk as students slowly moved from their seats and began looking for others with same colored notebooks. He watched as the more extroverted students led out, taking initiative with each other, while the more introverted students held back, waiting to be invited in.

Were there any diamonds in the rough here, he wondered. *A future Whitman, Dickens or Bronte? Maybe a King, Koontz, or Angelo?* He scanned the room with anticipation, feeling the same hopeful surge within him that always arrived on the first day of a new class. No matter how much he wanted to be in Ireland with his beautiful bride, he couldn't help being excited about the possibilities that each of these sixteen students carried within them.

CHAPTER THREE
MR. MONAHAN

ORLANDO LOOKED FOR OTHER BLUE FOLDERS. He saw the first in the hands of a sporty Asian girl. Jerking his head up in a nod, he moved toward her.

"Hey, I'm Orlando."

"Hi, I'm Tiffany." She began moving four desks into a square facing toward each other.

Orlando stood, searching the room for more blue folders. A pale white girl, gothic from head to toe with her black clothes, black lipstick and thick black eyeliner, sat at her desk drawing on her blue notebook. He knew her type from school, *slacker!* Orlando hated being in groups where his grade depended on other people. There was always someone who didn't want to do any work – someone who dragged the group down – and he thought this girl was just the one to do it. He walked over and tapped on the desk. "You gonna join us?"

The girl raised her head slowly, not smiling. "Uh, yeah, I guess," she mumbled through her scowl, slowly rising and gathering her stuff.

Orlando rolled his eyes as he headed back to their desks. He knew this was going to be a long day. Then he saw a lanky black guy had joined their group. _At least I'm not the only guy._ Orlando nodded his head and the other boy tilted his head up in acknowledgement. When the girl in black joined them, the Blue Group was complete.

"Now," said Mr. Monahan from the front of the class, "in a minute I'm going to have you introduce yourselves, but first I'm going to model for you how I want you to do it. Each of you will have three minutes. It doesn't sound like much, but it's actually hard to fill three minutes of space. I want you to time each other. You can talk about anything you want, but the point is to tell your group mates something about yourself. You can talk about your families, things you like or don't like, what you'd rather be doing right now..." some students laughed as he continued. "Who would like to time me? Anyone have a timer on their phone?"

The African American boy next to Orlando raised his hand, pulling an iPhone from his book bag. Orlando felt a stab of jealousy. An iPhone! Who was he kidding? He just wanted a cell phone, period.

"Okay, what's your name?" asked Mr. Monahan.

"Tyrell."

"Okay, Tyrell, tell me when to start."

Orlando saw Tyrell's thumb tap around on the surface of his phone. "Ready... go," he said as he started the timer.

Mr. Monahan stood up, took a deep breath and began his monologue. Speaking slowly with great enunciation and emphasis, he moved, pacing back and forth in front of the classroom. "My name is Brian Michael Monahan. The first thing people notice about me is that I'm tall."

Freakishly huge actually, thought Orlando.

"I am 6 feet 5inches tall to be exact. I've been a teacher here at McQueen High School for four years. I normally teach Junior and Senior AP English, but I'm teaching this class to make a little extra money this summer."

I can relate to that, thought Orlando.

"I help with student government and I co-lead the Drama Department. We did a play called, *The Crucible* in the fall and our spring musical was *Once Upon a Mattress.* I'm married to my lovely wife, Sarah. We've been married for two years now. Sarah is," he hesitated a moment, "*was* a journalist for the *Reno Gazette Journal.* Unfortunately, because of budget cuts, she is now an unemployed journalist. We have three dogs named Bowie, Cassie and Floyd. They are all named after bands or singers: David Bowie, Mama Cass Elliot, and Pink Floyd. We also have a cat named Prince."

A girl near the front raised her hand. Mr. Monahan held up his hand in a stop motion, "Nope. No questions during this exercise. Only the person talking gets to talk. Trust me, there will be plenty of time for questions later."

Mr. Monahan leaned back against the desk and continued. "I love to ride my bike or my longboard to school." Two students from the yellow group broke out with affirmations of "cool" and "sweet" then turned to each other, smiling and bumping fists.

Skaters…more slackers, thought Orlando.

Mr. Monahan continued, smiling. "Our environment is very important to me so I leave my car at home whenever possible.

"This summer I'd rather be in Ireland researching my family's roots, but because of the current devaluation of the dollar, I'm here with you instead." He stopped and smiled at them as if to assure them that, although second best, they were still okay in his book. Standing, he said with energy, "One thing I do have to look forward to this summer, however, is Burning Man." At this Mr. Monahan was interrupted with some cat calls and whoops.

What? Thought Orlando, *a teacher who goes to Burning Man?*

"I see some of you are familiar with Burning Man. Has anyone been there?" He looked around the room. No hands were raised. "I thought not. Well, for the uninformed, Burning Man is an annual arts festival in the Nevada desert. It happens once each year for a week and over 50,000 people come from all over America and many other countries to attend. This giant arts festival culminates with the burning of 'the man,' a forty-foot sculpture made of wood and steel.

"Sarah and I go to Burning Man to work as Rangers, which are volunteers who help anyone getting overheated, lost, injured, or over-indulging in illegal substances." Several of the students grinned or snickered at this comment.

That would be almost everybody there, thought Orlando.

"Yes, there are many at Burning Man who attend for reasons other than art. We also stay for a week after the event is over to help clean up the desert. The organization's pledge is to 'leave no trace.' So everything brought into the desert must be taken out."

That's kinda cool, thought Orlando.

"Burning Man takes place on a vast dry lake bed in the Black Rock Desert called the playa. This huge playa is covered in a fine dust which is very alkaline. It keeps anything from growing. So, there are no living things, besides people, at Burning Man. No bugs, no plants. Even birds fly around the playa because nothing grows for them to eat. And this alkali dust covers the cars and people, too. Have you seen the cars in town after Burning Man?" Most students nodded their heads.

Orlando had seen the burners' cars around town. They looked like they'd been uncovered from being buried for a hundred years.

"Well, this dust covers everyone's bodies, too, which helps keep the sun off your skin so you don't get sunburned. And it keeps the smell down, if you know what I mean!" This time there was general laughter in the room.

Sick! Thought Orlando. Running around in the hot sun covered in dust did not sound appealing to him. *But, they say the girls are sometimes naked...*

"Time!" interrupted Tyrell.

"There, you see?" said Mr. Monahan. "You can find out quite a lot about someone in three minutes. Now it's your turn. Choose someone from your group to be the timer. Other than timing, all cell phones should be on vibrate or turned off, please. Let's get started!"

CHAPTER FOUR
TIFFANY CHO

TIFFANY SAT IN SILENCE AS THE BLUE GROUP members shifted in their seats. She noticed Orlando looked uncomfortable with the tension of waiting and he spoke first.

"Well, maybe we should at least say our names first," he volunteered. "My name's Orlando Bustios." He looked to his left at the white girl wearing all black.

The girl raised her eyes from a detailed drawing on her notebook cover. "Sam Brown," her voice came out in a soft whisper. She continued drawing.

Tiffany sat up, leaned forward and smiled. "I'm Tiffany Cho."

The lanky black boy added with a guarded look, "And I'm Tyrell Dupree."

"Okay," said Orlando, "who wants to go first?"

The group fell silent. Tiffany squirmed in her seat. She remembered the promise she'd made in the car that morning, the promise to let herself be who she really was – who she wanted to be anyway. She was going to be free to express her opinions and reject the natural reserve that came from her culture. When she'd made the commitment this morning, she had had no idea the opportunity would come so quickly. Now that it was here, she felt shy and embarrassed. Taking a deep breath, she said "I'll go," before she could stop herself.

"I'll time," offered Tyrell, resetting his phone's timer.

Tiffany took another deep breath, trying to still her shaking hands, and began. "My name is Tiffany Cho. Well, actually, that's my American name. I was born Min-Gee Cho. Min-Gee means 'cleverness and wisdom,' but before my brother and I started school, we got to pick American names and I picked Tiffany. I kept Min-Gee for my middle name."

Tiffany felt like an idiot.Why had she shared that? What would these kids care about Korean names? She studied her group mates. Orlando was the easiest to read. He nodded and smiled at her encouragingly. Tyrell lounged back in his chair, stretching out his long legs, his face unreadable. Sam never looked up at Tiffany, just kept doodling on the cover of her blue folder. Tiffany reminded herself of her commitment not to hold back. Nervously, she went on, "Now that I'm older, I'm not sure it was a good pick. I kind of like the name Lauren or maybe Taylor better. They seem to fit me."

This feels so weird, thought Tiffany, *talking to people that can't talk back!* She continued, "So, I'm fifteen. I'm from a Korean family, obviously. My parents moved here to give us a better life. In Korea, my father was an engineer and my mother was a teacher, but when they came here they used all their savings to open a dry cleaning business. Now they own a chain of dry cleaners. My grandparents live with us and – "

Tyrell interrupted, "which cleaners?"

"No questions," Orlando said brusquely.

"Well," continued Tiffany, "it's the New Mikado cleaners. Anyway, my mom and dad aren't too happy being in the cleaning business, and they want me to be a doctor. So I feel a lot of pressure to do well in school." Not sure what else to say, Tiffany's voice trailed off and she turned to Tyrell, "How much longer do I have?"

He consulted his phone, "two more minutes."

"Man, this does go by slowly," she sighed. "Sooo, I have a brother named Hanju. He'll be a freshman this year. He's one of those perfect kids, good grades, blah, blah, blah. He even chose to keep his Korean name. I'm hoping he'll decide to be a doctor to take the pressure off me. I'd rather be a professional tennis player." Just the thought of this made Tiffany smile. She went on with more energy.

"I play on the tennis team at Reno High School. I love sports of any kind, though soccer, volleyball and tennis are my favorites. I won't really have a summer break 'cause I have to be here and then we start up tennis practice early, so no big summer plans."

Tiffany realized this was easier than she'd thought. She looked around at their faces; they were waiting eagerly for her to continue. These kids didn't think she was strange for wanting to play sports. Encouraged, she went on. "I have two dogs. They're poodles 'cause poodles don't shed and they can be around the dry cleaners. The white one is a girl. Her name is Gina, which in Korean means 'lovely,' and the brown one is a boy named Anto, which in Korean means 'big boy.' He's actually the same size as Gina, but anyway…"

Tiffany looked at Tyrell again. This time he was staring at her with interest. Her face grew hot. *Why do I always blush when boys look at me that way*, she wondered. Weakly she asked, "How much more time?"

Tyrell glanced at his phone, "about 45 seconds, but talk more about being Korean, it's interesting."

Her eyes widened and she sat up straighter. Being Korean was about the last thing she wanted to talk about, but this guy was cute!

"Well, being Korean is good and bad. There's a lot of pressure to succeed. That's why I'm in this class. My parents want me to start my sophomore year ahead in credits."

Tiffany had never thought much about *being* Korean before. She didn't feel very Korean, or very American for that matter. She felt slightly out of place in both worlds.

What else can I say?

Continuing the best she could, "I like Korean food. I like to have my relatives around, though many of them don't speak good English and my Korean is at elementary school level so... that's kinda awkward. We go to this Korean Presbyterian Church and the services are in Korean so I mostly tune out.

"I guess I'm not a good Korean. I mean, I'm not like, you know, what the good Korean would look like, or act like I guess. I'm kinda loud and kinda sporty and not really the ideal Korean woman, if you know what I mean. Since I was little I was a tomboy and my parents aren't happy about that. But I guess I like who I am. Weird thing, though, sometimes I forget I'm not white."

This last sentence had slipped out before Tiffany realized what she was saying. She felt her cheeks grow hot again. All three faces were now focused on her. Orlando let out an uncomfortable laugh. She even felt Sam look up, though Tiffany did not risk a glance at her. *Why did I say that?* Her face burned with shame.

She seemed to have an irrepressible desire to share herself with these people and had no idea why. It seemed like once she started saying these things out loud – things she'd only ever said to herself – the words kept tumbling out and she couldn't stop – she didn't want to. What she wanted to share next was pretty private. In fact, she was not sure she had ever spoken it out loud to anyone, but it was burning to get out of her now. She took a deep breath and began.

"What I mean is, I go to a pretty white school, and all my friends are white, and I just feel like them in every way. But, then sometimes I'll pass a mirror and be shocked by the girl in the mirror. And it takes me a minute, you know, to realize that the Asian girl in the mirror is me."

There was silence at the table for a moment as each member seemed to consider Tiffany's words. Strangely, she felt relieved. Tyrell glanced down and jerked his head up.

"Time! Sorry, I forgot to pay attention. You went a few seconds over."

Tiffany smiled nervously. "That's okay, I'm just glad to be done. That was the longest three minutes of my life!"

CHAPTER FIVE
TYRELL DUPREE

MR. MONAHAN HAD BEEN AMBLING around the room during Tiffany's speaking time, listening to each group's sharing. Now he stopped at the Blue Group's desks, "Everything going okay?" he asked.

"Yes," volunteered Orlando. "Tiffany just finished and we're ready to start round two."

Tyrell asked, "Can we ask questions once a person is done?"

"Not now," said Mr. Monahan. He looked up from Tyrell and addressed the group, "Trust me, we'll have plenty of time for questions. Today is only for uninterrupted sharing. How often do you get a chance to talk for three minutes without being interrupted?"

The group members considered the question, but no one spoke up. Finally, Tyrell answered, "Never I guess."

"That's right," said Mr. Monahan. "We live in a society where the ability to listen to each other, really listen, has been lost. So let's keep going. Who's next?"

Sam looked down at her at her notebook and Orlando and Tyrell looked at each other.

"I'll go," said Tyrell. "Will you time me?" he asked Orlando.

"Sure," Orlando took the phone.

Tyrell pointed out the stopwatch feature on his phone. "Just push "start" when you're ready for me to begin."

"Ready, go!" said Orlando, banging his finger down on the phone to press a button.

"Hey, lighten up!" snapped Tyrell, a bit too aggressively.

Orlando jerked his hand away from the phone. Tyrell saw the embarrassment on Orlando's face and lowered his voice, "The phone's face is sensitive to the electrostatic energy from your finger so you don't have to push on it like that. Just tap it lightly."

"Sorry," said Orlando sheepishly.

"It's okay, I'll start. My name is Tyrell Jovan Dupree. I'm a third generation Nevadan, which as you probably know, is a rarity. I go to Hug High School."

Tyrell's voice had a deep resonance. He spoke in smooth tones and enunciated each word carefully, just like his father did when he was preaching. It pleased him that because of this, people thought he was much older than his sixteen years.

Tyrell continued, "My father is a preacher. Well, actually, all the men in my family are preachers. I guess you could say I come from a long line of preachers. But the line stops with me. I am going to be a research scientist and I am going to find a cure for cancer."

Tyrell noticed Tiffany had reacted to his announcement with shock. Was she in shock that he knew he was going to find a cure for cancer, or that a black guy was interested in science? Wasn't science the thing most Asians studied? Yet, Tiffany had said she was more interested in sports. Tyrell shook off his thoughts and continued. "I'm sixteen. I have three older sisters, Shaundell, Rachell, and Machell. My parents wanted all of our names to end in -ell." Tyrell's head tilted to the right thoughtfully, "I'm not sure why. My sisters are really good singers and sing in our church and all over town whenever there is a gospel choir or something like that. I don't sing."

Tyrell's tall frame was still, brown eyes glazing over as he sank deep into thought. He was vaguely aware that Orlando and Tiffany were shifting uncomfortably at his long silence. He tended to take the time he needed to compose his thoughts, so when he started talking again it was as if nothing unusual had happened. This was another trait he shared with his father, and Tyrell felt it was an indication of hidden wisdom.

"My mother plays the piano and is musically gifted, teaching music at TMCC."

Orlando held up a finger, "Where?" he asked.

"Truckee Meadows Community College," Tyrell answered. "She has a Master's degree in Music Education from UNR." He glanced at Orlando and clarified, "University of Nevada, Reno."

Orlando rolled his eyes.

"Sorry, I guess everyone knows what UNR is. Anyway, Dad left Reno for college, graduating with a Master's in Philosophy from Brown University. That's where he met my mom when she was getting her undergraduate degree in Education. Brown University is in Rhode Island and I'm going to go there. I'll be the third generation in my family to go to Brown because Grandpa went there, too. They have an excellent research program. And that is why I'm taking this class. I'm going to be a junior, but I'm not as good at English as I am at Science, and I need to get my grade up from the 'C' I got in this class last year."

The blonde girl, Sam, actually made a noise at this comment. It was an odd little noise, like a puff of air that escaped accidently. It was as if she'd been holding her breath and it all suddenly puffed out in a huff. Tyrell wondered if she was mocking him and suddenly felt angry. This was not unusual as anger was never far from his surface. He looked at Sam, who did not raise her eyes from her drawing. That glance diverted his anger as he noticed the picture she was drawing was really quite good. It was a medieval sketch of a dragon rearing on its hind legs with a knight in armor standing below, holding a sword. Tyrell wondered at how quickly his moods could change. First, he'd been angry; now he was curious.

"Wow," Tyrell said to Sam with sincere admiration, "you are an excellent artist!"

Sam raised her face to Tyrell. "Thanks," she said dismissively, looking down quickly. Tyrell leaned over Orlando's desk and checked the clock. "Only 15 seconds left." His time was passing by and yet he hadn't said that much. Was there anything else he could say? Tiffany had been so open in her sharing. Should he should follow her example? What would be the point? He'd never see these kids again and yet, he felt a growing desire to try an experiment. His classmates were not all white, as he'd originally thought. What would it be like to try to know people outside of his own safe circle? It would be like a social experiment. He decided he had nothing to lose so he launched in.

"Tiffany shared something honest about herself, and although I've never mistaken myself for being white, I admire her honesty." He sent a dazzling smile toward Tiffany, which she returned. "So, I will share something personal about myself as well. I told you that I come from a family of preachers, right?" Tiffany and Orlando nodded at Tyrell and Sam looked up from her drawing. "Well," Tyrell looked each one in the eye before continuing, "I am an atheist." He concluded with this statement and sat still, watchful.

Finally, Orlando glanced at the phone. "Time."

CHAPTER SIX
ORLANDO BUSTIOS

"**N**OW DO YOU WANT ME TO TIME YOU?" Tyrell asked Orlando. "Oh, okay."

He handed the phone back to Tyrell who expertly tapped the screen a few times and then said, "Go."

Orlando sat up straighter in his chair. He was not tall and lanky like Tyrell. His body was shorter and more compact, his skin a deep brown. His face was serious as he cleared his throat and began, "My name is Orlando Tomas Oscar Bustios," he said with a proud Spanish flourish. "I don't really know what my name means. I do know I was named after Oscar Romero, the one good Archbishop in El Salvador, and after my uncle Tomas.

"I like to play video games. I play video games most of the time. I'm taking this class to improve my English score and get ahead for next year. I live with my mom and my grandmother. They work at the Circus Circus Casino." Orlando was silent. Then, "I really don't know what else to say. I'm fifteen and I go to Wooster High School."

Tiffany piped up, "Tell us about where your family is from. Is it El Salvador?" Orlando frowned, thoughtfully. This felt like a sensitive subject to him. But Tiffany and Tyrell had shared personal things. Maybe he would share a little bit with them. If nothing else, he thought, it would please his mother to find out that he'd spoken about his heritage in class. "Yes, my family is from El Salvador. My family lived in El Salvador during terrible times. My grandfather, uncle Tomas, and older brothers were killed by soldiers. My grandmother somehow brought my mother and me to the U.S. They escaped before I was born."

Orlando was quiet for a minute trying to decide what to share. The rest was really private. He did not want to tell them everything. He decided to stick to safer topics. All eyes were on him and he lifted his chin toward Tyrell and Tiffany. "You have both talked about your religious backgrounds. This is a hard subject for my family. We used to be Catholic but the Catholic Church, mostly anyway, supported the army and my family did not. The soldiers were the real thugs in El Salvador. They came to our village on American-built trucks and used American-made weapons to murder us. It is hard for us to be in America knowing that. It is also hard to be Catholic. Our family is nothing now, no faith or religion, just," he sighed before continuing, "our family. We just believe in ourselves."

Orlando listened to himself speaking and thought about what the others must hear. He had a slight Latino accent in spite of being raised in America. He knew that his accent mostly came from talking with his *Abuela*. In other classes he'd tried to practice hiding his accent, but he decided not to worry about that right now.

"I'd like to get a job that pays a lot of money so I can take care of my mom and my grandmother. Maybe I'll be in business or computers. Maybe I'll make video games." He smiled at the thought. "I don't know. I am sure I'll *never* work in a casino."

He paused for breath. "How much time left?"

Tyrell glanced at his phone, "About thirty seconds."

Orlando began again, "We don't have any pets. I don't have any brothers or sisters that are living. Uh, this is hard to think of something to say. We live in an apartment…"

Tiffany leaned in toward him, "Tell us something nobody else knows. You know, like Tyrell and I did."

Orlando was quiet for a long time, thinking. What could he share with these strangers? Tyrell seemed so sure of himself and Tiffany was assertive and honest; what did he have to say? He really didn't want to share anything personal. They didn't know anything about him, yet they'd been honest with him. It didn't make sense.

Maybe this is my chance to make some friends, he realized. He'd never really had close friends in his life. He lived in a dangerous neighborhood where gangs were constantly recruiting. His mother made him stay close to home, so mostly, he played video games. *What would it be like to have friends?* Would sharing something personal bring these people closer, or scare them away?

He decided to say something few people knew; if he didn't make friends with these people, at least they didn't go to his school. "My mother was thirty years old when the soldiers came. They killed my grandfather and my uncle and my brothers in front of my grandmother and mother. Then they raped them both."

Nobody in the Blue Group moved. Each seemed stunned at Orlando's revelations. Orlando glanced at Sam and was shocked to see her face showed tears running over her thick makeup. He hadn't expected that. What were they thinking? How to switch groups without hurting his feelings? They didn't even know his family, why should they care so much? Orlando felt the deep pain in his chest he always felt when he thought about what had happened to his family. *This was why some things should stay secret,* he thought, *this is why I've never shared it before.*

Finally, Tyrell tore his eyes away from Orlando and looked down at his phone, "Time."

Orlando felt cut off, embarrassed. He began to feel his face growing hot and wondered if he should try to find a way to drop the class. He had shared too much. Mr. Monahan's words broke into his misery.

"Most of you," he began as he walked up to the front of the room, "have completed the third round. Before we begin round four, raise your hands and tell me some of your thoughts about this exercise in listening." Hands flew up all around the room. He continued, "Hands down for a minute. Now, I don't want to hear anything that was shared in your groups. These groups are sacred space. What you share in them is not for anyone outside of your group to hear. They need to be a safe space for you. I'll be sharing in your stories vicariously as I read your journals, but other than that, we must all keep confidentiality, okay?"

He looked around the room for definite nods of agreement before he went on.

"What I want you to tell me is this: how does talking for three minutes uninterrupted feel? What is it like to open your soul like that? And, on the other hand, what is it like to listen to someone else's story without asking questions?"

Hands were raised more slowly this time. A red-haired girl near the front said, "I think it's really hard to not ask questions. I mean, the people in my group are really interesting and there's so much I want to know."

"Yes," replied Mr. Monahan glancing at his class list on the desk. "You're Becca, right?" The redhead nodded.

"I know it's really frustrating. But as I asked the Blue Group earlier, when was the last time you talked to anyone for three minutes without being interrupted?"

The students were quiet in their seats, thoughtful.

"Never?" Becca said, her voice going up at the end of the word, as if she'd never thought of this before.

Mr. Monahan explained, "That's because we live in a world that has lost the art of listening. We have more means of communication available to us than any other generation, and yet, we rarely take our eyes off our phones and computers long enough to really hear each other. And listening is how we learn about what's important to someone. In a practical way, it's how we love."

There was an uncomfortable shifting at the word "love."

"Oh, come on," said Mr. Monahan. "There's nothing embarrassing about loving each other. If we were better listeners we'd be better friends and there would be less war and, yes, we'd be better lovers too!"

There were snickers from the class at this.

"So," he continued, "Any other comments, especially about the sharing process?"

One of the skater boys Orlando had noticed earlier raised his hand. Mr. Monahan glanced at his desk again, "Yes, Joshua?"

Joshua talked fast and loud, as if used to commanding attention, "It's just dang hard to talk that long!" The class laughed loudly.

He's like a cartoon character, thought Orlando.

"Ah," said Mr. Monahan, "an astute observation, anyone else?"

Tyrell's hand went up next to Orlando. Orlando gripped the edge of his desk and sunk into his chair. With a glance at the desktop class list, Mr. Monahan said, "Tyrell?"

"I'm impressed with the level of sharing in our group. We've known each other less than an hour but it seems that we've been together a lot longer."

Orlando looked at Tyrell with astonishment. Tyrell's face looked sincere and positive. He turned to Tiffany and Sam to see that they were nodding in agreement. Tiffany had a wide, warm smile on her face, and Sam was still staring at her notebook, but her tears had been wiped away. He noticed Sam's black eyeliner was no longer neat, and some of it had come off on her hand. Orlando felt relieved; maybe he hadn't shared too much. Or, maybe he had, but they weren't scared away. Maybe, sharing that you forgot you were Korean or that you were a secret Atheist was just as scary to them.

Mr. Monahan smiled hugely. "Now, that's what I want to hear. Excellent! It sounds like your group is taking risks: sharing things that really matter. Okay, now let's get back to our last person and finish up this assignment."

CHAPTER SEVEN
SAM BROWN

A LL EYES OF THE BLUE GROUP MEMBERS turned toward Sam.
"I'll clock you," said Tyrell. He got his timer ready and,
without waiting for her assent, said, "Go."

Sam blew out a long breath that made her bangs flutter off her
forehead, but they fell back immediately. *What am I supposed to say
to this group of babblers?* She'd been shocked how much had been
shared so far. She was not going to tell anything personal to total
strangers, *that* was for sure. They were all looking at her and she
began to chatter nervously, her voice soft but clear. "Have you guys
ever been in the hospital where you have to stay overnight?" She saw
each shake their head no.

"Well this," she said waving her hand at their group, "is just
about what it's like. I had my tonsils out when I was twelve and I
had to stay overnight because they wouldn't stop bleeding. There was
another girl in the room with me, and even though we'd never met,
it was dark and we were scared and we ended up talking all night.
It was really weird because it was like we'd become best friends, but
then in the morning when I went home we never saw each other
again. Kinda like now. This whole thing will be done in four weeks
and then what?"

Three sets of eyes watched her as she paused after this odd beginning. She realized that in her nervousness, she'd varied from the script they had all followed. "Okay, I'll start again," she said. "My name is Samantha Ashley Brown. I'm sixteen and I'm going to be a junior at McQueen next year. I'm taking this class over 'cause I flunked it last year." As she said this she looked at Tyrell with a challenge in her eye. "I don't really like school," she continued.

"I live with my mom and her most recent husband, Dirk. I have a half-sister named Charity and," she said with resignation, "I have to watch her a lot. She's seven." Sam stiffened, defensively, with her chin up, as if someone had insulted her sister. "She's alright. It's just a pain to have to watch her all the time."

Sam could read Tiffany's face easily. Tiffany obviously thought she was a freak. *Whatever,* thought Sam, *I don't need her to like me. I just need to get through this.* She started again.

"I like art," she held up her notebook. It was now completely covered with a detailed drawing of a knight fighting a dragon while a skinny girl in tattered clothes hid low in the corner of the page. "I don't draw specific themes, just whatever comes to mind."

"That's amazing," said Orlando.

Tiffany's nose wrinkled as if the drawing smelled bad to her.

"Art is my favorite class at school. I have a really cool art teacher. If it wasn't for her, I'd drop out tomorrow. She lets me work in her room to earn extra credit. I'm her TA." She stopped and looked at Tyrell, "how much time?"

Tyrell glanced at his phone, "About a minute and a half."

"Wow," Sam said, "this *is* harder than it looks." She regarded her group members. What did they want from her? Maybe she would throw them a bone. Let them think she was being open with them. She decided to shock them a little.

"Well, I've lived in lots of different places. My mom likes to move about as much as she likes to get married. I've been to three high schools, two middle schools, four elementary schools, and one juvenile detention center." The looks she got from "detention center" were exactly what she'd hoped for, but somehow it wasn't satisfying. "That makes it a bit hard to make friends," she concluded.

Again, Tiffany's face mirrored disapproval. *She probably thinks I don't have any friends because I'm a freak. But I don't have any friends because I don't want any!* What else could she say? She decided to switch to sympathy instead of shock. Shock was too easy and she would have to talk to these people, like, every day.

"My mom is on her fourth marriage. I have two half-brothers who live with their dad – father number two – and two step-brothers that live with their mom in Idaho from Dirk, my current stepdad. Charity is from father number three, who is in jail where he belongs."

She added the last part of this sentence with finality, slamming the jail door with her words. Sam saw Tiffany's eyebrows raise with concern. Tyrell's face didn't change but he sat straighter in his seat. Orlando's bittersweet expression read pain and concern. He felt sorry for her, but he wanted her to go on. Sympathy felt uncomfortable, Sam realized. *Enough of that,* she thought, moving away from the subject of her nightmares to something lighter.

"My favorite color is black. Before we moved here, I had a room that I painted black with glow-in-the-dark pictures painted on it. No one could see the pictures unless it was dark. I really, really liked that room."

Tiffany leaned in a little closer as a half-smile crept in the corner of her mouth. She seemed to survey Sam's all-black outfit. Sam could tell Tiffany was somehow softening to her a little. Sam didn't want Tiffany to soften. Trusting people was a weakness. She's learned that all weaknesses were exploited in one way or another. Then again, what did she expect? She *had* played the sympathy card.

To hell with their reactions, she thought, *let's just get this over with.* She started to rattle off disconnected facts. "I had two dogs, one in Idaho and one we got in Fallon, but we had to get rid of them when we moved. Our new apartment doesn't allow pets." After saying this, Sam leaned over to glance at Tyrell's phone. It read ten seconds.

How could she end this thing in a way that seemed to be sharing something vulnerable but was really just a cover? She decided to go for shock value again.

"And, the thing that not many people know about me is, I put father number three in jail. He is in jail now, where I hope he dies."

CHAPTER EIGHT
THE DREAM

TYRELL NOTICED THE SECOND DAY of English class was completely different from the first. On the first day the students slouched into the room, sad to be up early during what should have been summer vacation. Today they bounced in with more energy. Students, who had met each other only yesterday, were clustered in groups and chatting. Mr. Monahan had to clear his throat to get them to be quiet.

"Morning class!" he said. "You all look marvelous this sunny June morning!"

Several students smiled up at him as he added, "Is anyone missing from your groups?" Tyrell looked at his three group mates. All three met his gaze in a way that suggested they were no longer strangers. He nodded. Students from other groups did the same.

"Great!" he said. "Then we will jump right in! Last night your assignment was to journal in response to the question: 'What's been bugging you lately?' Now since it's one of those fabulous Reno mornings, and it isn't snowing this week, I have a surprise for you." Several students laughed.

Mr. Monahan was interrupted by a raised hand. It was a chubby girl in the Red Group. He glanced down at his desk notes, "Chandra?"

She spoke in a surprisingly gravelly voice, as if she'd been smoking a long time. "Why would it be snowing in June?"

He smiled knowingly. "You're new here, aren't you?"

"Yes, we just moved here from San Diego."

"Ah," he said wistfully, "from paradise to Reno, Nevada. I'm so sorry." More students laughed.

Tyrell understood the inside joke. His aunt had once lived in San Diego, which was lush and green, and Reno was, well…brown.

"Well," he continued, "Chandra, Reno's weather is… shall we say, unpredictable. You see, we are actually a desert, but high desert. We're at about forty-five hundred feet here. So normally we'd be a cold, wet place instead of a desert. But unfortunately for us, as the rain clouds rise up high to go over the Sierra Nevada range, they drop most of the water in California, leaving us with beautiful but empty clouds. We are in what is called a 'rain shadow.' We're still high up and sometimes the moisture makes it over the mountain, but at the most unpredictable of moments, we've had snow in July before."

At this, Chandra's eyes got large. "No way!" she said loudly in her gravelly voice.

"Way. Don't feel bad, Chandra. Most people in Reno are from somewhere else. Does anyone here have advice about living in Reno for Chandra?"

Tyrell put his hand up immediately as hands went up all over the room. Picking up his clipboard, Mr. Monahan began to call names, "Amy?"

The statuesque African-American girl spoke in a quiet voice, "Buy some Chapstick."

Heads nodded in agreement around the room and Tyrell and two others put their hands down. They'd wanted to offer the same advice because Reno was so dry. Tyrell licked his lips at the reminder.

"Toby?" Mr. Monahan called.

One of the two skater boys answered, "Drink a lot of water." Again, knowing heads nodded and two more hands went down.

"Okay, one last hand," said Mr. Monahan. "Tiffany?"

Tyrell turned to look at Tiffany, his heartbeat quickening a little. It was like she was a friend and he was excited to see what she would say. Tyrell chuckled to himself quietly. How strange.

Tiffany smiled, "Wear layers!" The class seemed to agree.

"It's true," added Mr. Monahan. "San Diego is a sunny seventy-five degrees most days, but Reno is one of those, 'if you don't like the weather, wait a minute' places. Okay, enough on Reno for now. Your surprise is, I want you to read your journal entries to each other outside today."

A cheer echoed around the room and happy students nodded and smiled at each other.

Mr. Monahan continued, "You have one hour, so be back here at nine-fifteen. Out you go," he paused, then added, "oh, and Chandra, one more thing, wear sunscreen. When the sun is out, it can burn you quick!"

He smiled at them as they gathered their backpacks and notebooks. "Wait, wait," he said quickly. Tyrell stopped. "I want you to read what you've written, then give the group some time to respond. They can ask questions, and they can share similar experiences or maybe offer advice. Somebody keep time so every person gets a chance to share. You should have fifteen minutes each," he clarified as they began to file out of the room and down the metal steps leading to McQueen High School's asphalt parking lot.

Tyrell surveyed the landscape in front of him. It was strange to leave a classroom and be outside without having to navigate hallways first. His school didn't have portable classrooms. He understood they were added for overflow students. Maybe more kids wanted to go to McQueen than to his high school – that wouldn't really surprise him.

He looked across the parking lot, which stretched out before him as long as a football field. On the other side were hills of grass and trees that ascended to the main campus. He noticed the sharp staircase in the middle of the grass that would carry students to and from their classes in the main campus down to the parking lot where he stood. *I wouldn't want to climb those everyday.*

Tyrell suggested a spot on a grassy knoll across the parking lot from the portable and they all walked that way. It was probably the closest green spot and a lot of the other students were headed in the same direction but veered off to different sections as they got closer.

The groups scattered along the soft slope that defined the back side of the high school. Although the parking lot and its manicured lawns were the first thing you saw when you drove up to the school, the actual entrance to the school was way around the opposite side of the building. What seemed like the front of the school was really the back.

As Tyrell pondered this oddity, they all sat down. *Strange,* he realized, *most of these kids will never see the front of this school. They'll only know the back parking lot and the cheap-looking portables.* He knew this from driving around to find his class the first day. He wondered if Sam thought about it. Would she want people to see the front of her school? Did she even like school? At least this one had grass. His school seemed to be planted on old concrete.

Tiffany interrupted his thoughts, "Who should start?"

Tyrell noticed that they all glanced down, looking a bit shy after sharing so much of themselves the day before. He opened his mouth, but Orlando beat him to it, "Why don't we just go around like yesterday?"

No one objected.

Tiffany's voice squeaked, "Ok, then I'm first." Her hands shook as she grabbed her journal out of her blue and white book bag with the large white Nike symbol.

Tyrell wondered why she looked so tense as she opened her notebook.

"What's that on your cover?" Sam asked, pointing to a sticker that said "Yonex".

"Oh," replied Tiffany flipping to the front of the notebook. "It's my favorite racquet brand. I got a Yonex for Christmas this year. It's awesome!" Tiffany looked around the group, but when no one commented, she turned her gaze to the notebook, disappointment glazing her face.

"Let me say before I begin," she looked up with revived energy. "I'm so glad we get to be outside. I just can't stand being indoors during the summer. Well, I can't really stand it in the winter either, but it's harder in the summer."

If it was my choice we'd be inside, thought Tyrell. He'd never been the outdoorsy type or athletic. He preferred a quiet room for reading over a basketball game at the park.

Tiffany took a breath and began to read. "What bugs me most is I don't ever seem good enough for my parents."

The first line grabbed Tyrell's attention. *That's sad,* he thought. He'd always felt love and acceptance from his parents. He wondered if that would change when he told them what he'd been thinking about lately, about what he'd decided. He pictured their normally lively dinners turning stone silent. He pictured his family leaving for church on Sundays without him. He was surprised to feel a wave of loss wash over him.

Tiffany read, "This is how it happened. After school I was thinking about what we talked about in our group today. I really liked hearing everyone's stories and everything. It made me think we're all the same, really, but with different problems and everything. So, I guess I was feeling kinda glad I don't have some of the problems my group members do. I was feeling grateful, I guess, for my own set of problems.

"But then, we had dinner and my Mom asked about class. I said I really liked it because we got to share in our group, and I got to know a lot about each person in my group. Then my mom had a cow. She went off about how she was paying good money for this class and why wasn't I learning about English? Why were we wasting time 'sharing?' She went on a rant that covered my educational failings, the educational failings in our local schools, and America's educational policies. I mean nobody was left untouched. This is why I don't share with my parents. What's the point?"

Tyrell noticed that Tiffany was beginning to get louder as she spoke and she wasn't reading anymore, just telling the story. But her eyes never left the notebook. He felt bad for her.

She said, "I know my life looks pretty sweet compared to some people's lives in my group. Maybe I'm shallow and ungrateful but this really, really bugs me." Tiffany stopped and looked up around the group, her face shiny with sweat.

Tyrell spoke first. "What did you say to your mom?"

"Oh, you can't say anything when my mom gets on a rant! You just sit there quietly until she's done and then pray your brother says something stupid that gets the focus off of you."

"How long does she talk for?" asked Orlando.

Tiffany rolled her eyes. "Well, that depends on what the issue is. I mean, this was a relatively minor issue, so it lasted about ten minutes. But if it was something epic, like why I don't want to be a doctor, it goes on for weeks. And then just when you think it's blown over, Mom starts up again with more arguments or guilt or whatever she can think of to try to press her point. Then she starts enlisting the relatives! My mom and grandmother don't agree on much, but on this point they are absolutely on the same team"

Tyrell wondered what it would be like to live in a household with so much strife. Was that what his house would be like when he told his parents that he didn't believe in God? *No,* he concluded, *they might not agree with me, they might even be really disappointed in me, but they would never treat me like that.*

"What's her point?" asked Orlando.

"Her 'point,'" began Tiffany, her voice getting higher and speech faster, "is that I'm not good enough. Or that my goals, hopes and dreams aren't good enough. I have to have *her* goals, *her* hopes and *her* dreams. She wanted to be a teacher and not run a dry cleaning business, but her license doesn't work in America and her English isn't good enough. She felt saddled with the cleaners the first day they bought it. She is bitter about it and wants to live through me.

"I'm sick of it! It's like they don't even see me anymore. It's like my job is to carry my mom's *Han*, her pain, and I don't want to do it anymore. They only see what they want to see; what they want me to be."

She stopped talking, breathing hard. She had been pulling on the grass around her as she spoke, and it was scattered across her legs and notebook. "Sorry guys," she said sheepishly, looking down. "Guess I'm the one on a rant now."

"You should just ignore her," suggested Sam. "That's what I do. I just put in my ear buds and tune them out."

Tiffany looked at Sam as if she just walked out of a spaceship. "Uh, that wouldn't work in my house. Korean kids aren't exactly allowed to 'tune out' their parents."

"Really?" said Sam in disbelief. "I'd tune 'em out. I don't care what country they're from."

Tyrell saw an understanding look pass between Tiffany and Orlando. He wondered about it. He thought about Sam's cavalier response. He knew if he ignored his parents he'd at least get a reaction; maybe it would be one of his mother's withering looks, or a quick smack on the side of the head. His mother had no tolerance for disrespect from her children. Maybe Tiffany and Orlando had parents more like his than like Sam's.

They talked about ideas and strategies for Tiffany until her time was up. It was Tyrell's turn. He pulled out his notebook, wishing he hadn't written about what he had. *Oh, well, this is just an experiment, right?* He read, "What bugs me, is this dream I keep having."

All the members of the Blue Group seemed generally surprised by his opening sentence. Tyrell wondered why, they couldn't all write about their families could they? Or were they trying to keep from launching into Martin Luther King Jr. references? He smiled at the thought and prepared to disappoint them.

"It always starts the same way. I'm walking up this dark road and there are big trees lining the road, pine trees. There are cars going by and I'm kind of afraid. I see a sign up ahead for a rest stop and I know, I just know, that I'm supposed to go there. But I really don't want to. When I get there, there is a lane for cars and a lane for trucks. I'm supposed to go to the lane for trucks, though I don't know why. So I begin to head that way and as I do, my heart pounds harder and harder, and I know I'm looking for someone, a blonde girl. I know she's in danger, but I can't find her. I begin to run and there are lots of trucks, all parked close together, semi-trucks: some new, some old. None of them look the same. I look between each one, but I can't find her. I know I need to find her, to help her, but I can't! Then I wake up."

Tyrell looked up at the group staring silently back at him. He continued to read, "It's awful, and I have this dream almost every night. I wake up feeling panicky, with my heart racing. It's *really* starting to bug me."

He put down his notebook and looked at his group expectantly. They'd had a lot to say about Tiffany's problem, and this was so much simpler. Would they have any answers? He was getting desperate, desperate enough to share this dream with people he hardly knew. He waited hopefully.

"This is good," said Sam, looking perky for the first time since Tyrell had met her. "We can help you interpret the dream." She said this as if it were the easiest thing in the world to interpret a dream. As if it was something she did every day. Orlando and Tiffany looked at her with new interest.

Tyrell felt a little annoyed. There was no exact science to dream interpretation. Dream interpretation on an expert level would still depend on a psychologist, and psychology was a soft science. He didn't trust it. He did trust the more proven methods of sleep aids and relaxation practices, but he'd tried them and nothing kept the dream from waking him.

"You know how to do that?" asked Tiffany, much more excited about the idea of dream interpretation than Tyrell.

"Well, not exactly, but how hard can it be? Dreams are just our subconscious, our way of working out our problems, right?"

Tyrell suppressed a scoff. He studied Sam, his head tilted to the side as if seeing her for the first time. Where was all this *supposed* knowledge coming from? "Dreams," said Tyrell knowingly, "are just electronic impulses firing in your brain based on different factors, like what you ate for dinner."

"If you really believe that," challenged Sam, "then why is this dream freaking you so bad?" She looked him directly in the eyes for the first time.

Tyrell felt like he'd just been slapped. He realized that though Sam may have seemed quiet in class yesterday, she was definitely not a shy person. He had already asked himself this question a million times. If he believed dreams were just electronic impulses, then why *was* this dream bugging him so much? He'd even tried varying his before-bed meals to see if it made a difference. But he wouldn't admit that. "I don't know," he said sharply. "It's just that it's not like a regular dream. It seems real. And I wake up feeling like someone out there is in trouble, and I need to go help them."

"Well," said Sam, with even more energy, "let's suppose that the dream *is* your subconscious trying to tell you something. What could it be saying?"

They sat quietly for a moment. Tyrell tried to understand Sam's question.

Tiffany took a stab at it. "I think it would mean you are worried about something."

"No joke," said Orlando. Tyrell wondered if he was being sarcastic.

"That's it," said Sam. "Tiffany's got it. Obviously you're worried about something. You're searching and searching but you never find it. So, what is it?"

Tiffany, eyes wide, gaped at Sam.

Sam asked again, "Tyrell, what are you worried about?"

Tyrell grudgingly considered this question. What was he worried about? Being here with them for one thing, but there was no way he was going to say that. His grades, college, what wasn't he worried about? He finally decided to share his biggest concern of the moment. "The only thing I can think of is that I decided to tell my parents I'm not coming to church anymore. I'm going to tell them tonight and I'm not sure they'll take it very well."

"There!" said Sam. "You see, how easy that was?"

Orlando spoke up, "Well, I don't agree. That doesn't really seem to go with the dream. The dream is more like a movie, or a video game, where Tyrell has to rescue the princess!"

"Yeah, well, you can't take dreams literally," challenged Sam. "They're symbolic."

"How do you know so much about dreams?" demanded Orlando. He wanted to consider the princess idea a bit longer.

"I really like psychology...and I read a lot," Sam answered with hesitant pride.

They discussed the dream until Tyrell's time was up but made no conclusions.

Then it was Orlando's turn. He took out his notebook, his forehead creased in concentration. "What bugs me," he read, "is the welfare system. I hate it when people assume that my family is on welfare. They just assume because they think we're Mexican, and they think all Mexicans are on welfare. My grandma worked hard to become a citizen of the United States and she and my mother work very hard to pay our bills. We do not take welfare. I believe that any family who wants to should be able to work and not be on welfare. It's a crutch for so many people, and families like mine are judged because other people take advantage of it." He paused after finishing.

"I agree," said Tyrell.

"My family was on welfare a couple of times," said Sam defensively. "When we were between step-dads and it was just my mom, she got food stamps for us and Medicaid. Without it, we wouldn't have made it."

Orlando would not back down, "Well, I think that hard work is what makes America a strong nation. I don't agree with what Americans did in El Salvador, but I have to admit it's a great nation because the immigrants who have come here work hard. Your family is a good example, Sam. You said your family *was* on welfare, but they aren't anymore. They worked hard to get off it. That shows you are not abusers of the system. Immigrants who come here and get on welfare should have one year to get off and if they can't get off, they should be sent home."

"Well, what if they can't get off the system, if one is injured or disabled?" Sam challenged.

"Well, of course there are exceptions. I'm saying they should never stop trying – no one on Welfare can be truly free."

"Who are you to determine what makes people free?"

"I'm talking about what bugs me; it's my opinion," Orlando said and smiled.

Tyrell was surprised not only by Orlando's strong opinions, but also how clearly he articulated his thoughts. He had obviously discussed this before. He was also surprised by Sam. She didn't back down from Orlando either. They seemed to be enjoying their verbal sparring. Sam and Orlando bantered back and forth some more. Tiffany and he watched with interest. The debate swung back and forth between Orlando and Sam evenly. They both spoke passionately, but neither got angry or defensive. He noticed he would have been upset if it were he in Orlando or Sam's position. He didn't do well when he was challenged.

As their fifteen minutes drew to a close, Orlando and Sam easily let the topic drop. Then it was Sam's turn to read from her notebook. She flipped through the pages to find the assigned topic.

"What bothers me is school," Sam read.

Big surprise there, thought Tyrell.

"Why should I have to take classes I have no interest in and have no bearing on my life, like Math? I don't need math to be an artist, right? I hate taking classes that have no point in my life. It's ridiculous. Just because some big shot somewhere decided that all 'well-rounded' people have to know certain stuff, I can't spend my time studying the subjects I love and will actually spend my life pursuing. It's a flippin' waste of time and money."

"I agree," said Orlando. Sam and Orlando smiled at each other because they agreed so easily after spending so much time debating.

Tyrell looked at Orlando in shock. He didn't understand how Orlando could be completely comfortable arguing with Sam one minute and agreeing with her the next. These people were turning out to be more interesting than he thought. His head swiveled back and forth as Orlando and Sam debated. Sam's face was relaxed and she seemed to be enjoying herself as much as Orlando. Tiffany sat quietly but seemed as content to watch as much as Tyrell.

"I think the system they have for education in Europe is best," Orlando offered to the group. "There you have a choice about what you want to study after only two years in high school. You can focus on what you're really interested in."

Tyrell disagreed. He had thought about the subject before. His World History teacher made the class watch a documentary on the educational system in Japan. Students studied from early morning into the late evening, and then chose a specialty and entered it early. "One of the things that makes a country strong is having a broad-based education," he finally said. "I don't like taking English and

Grammar, but I understand English is necessary if I'm to be successful in an English-based society."

Tiffany chimed in, "I agree with Tyrell. For one thing, I don't even know what I want to study in college, so I think it's good to be exposed to lots of different things. If I got to choose, I'd just play sports all the time, and that wouldn't be best for me."

"Well, I don't plan to go to college," said Sam. "I'd like to get out of school as soon as possible."

They talked on until their group time ended. All in all, it was a stimulating discussion, Tyrell realized. He hadn't gotten upset when Sam and Orlando stuck to their opinion. They offered their points of view as just that, points of view. He also enjoyed their ability to articulate thoughts and share them with each other. At home, his family mostly talked over each other, instead of discussing a single topic together.

Tyrell packed up and headed to class. He felt they'd already done a full day's work. Walking down the hill together, he heard Tiffany say to Orlando, "Orlando, I think you should be a lawyer someday!"

"A lawyer? Why?"

"Well, you have a lot of strong opinions, and you explain them well. When you argue, it's like, not mean."

"What do you mean, not mean?"

"It's not mean, like some people. When they argue, they do it to hurt others, but with you it's more like, I don't know. It's just fun, I guess. You have a way of debating that is really interesting."

Orlando said, "I've never thought about that before."

Tyrell thought about Tiffany's observations as they walked across the parking lot. They were good ones. She had a lot of insight. Orlando *would* make a good lawyer. Tyrell glanced over at Orlando and noticed he was lost in thought, a smile playing on his lips.

CHAPTER NINE
THE ROOMS

THE THIRD DAY OF CLASS DAWNED WARM and clear. Tiffany stood outside the portable with her classmates. Most were in shorts and t-shirts, chatting and waiting for Mr. Monahan to open the door. Tiffany noticed two glaring exceptions to the warm weather clothes. Sam still wore long sleeves and pants, though the material of her black clothes was lighter weight. Leaning against the portable for warmth, shivering slightly in her sweater and pants stood Chandra, the girl from sunny California.

The door had always been unlocked when they'd arrived before. If Mr. Monahan was inside, he was not responding to Toby, who was pounding on the door. Tiffany looked up at a rush of sound as Mr. Monahan came around the corner on his longboard. He whooshed in among them, scattering students with his sudden approach. Hitting the end of the longboard with his toe, he flipped the other end up into his hand and grinned at them.

"Sorry, I'm late!" He rushed up the steps to unlock the door.

Sam, Tyrell, Tiffany and Orlando had been clustered together talking when Mr. Monahan arrived and now headed into the classroom.

"Is he limping?" asked Tyrell.

"Yeah, he is," responded Orlando.

I wonder what happened to him, thought Tiffany, *I hope he's okay.*

Inside the classroom, Mr. Monahan definitely moved slower than usual. Students commented to each other about this as he began moving things from his satchel to his desk. When the class was settled, he spoke. "So, you notice I'm not one hundred percent today?"

There was a general murmur of agreement. Toby spoke up, "What's wrong? Did you wreck your deck?"

"That's exactly what I did, Toby." Mr. Monahan held up his longboard and pointed to a, black gash on the underside. "See this? It wasn't here this morning. You know how I had you all write about a time when you felt embarrassed? Well, I was going to start with a story of my own from when I was in high school, but I have a much more current story now."

The classroom came alive as students shifted in anticipation.

"I was cruisin' down Robb Drive to the school and just got to the curb right in front of a city bus stop. Students were filing off the bus for school so I decided to ride up onto the sidewalk out of the street. But, instead of sliding gracefully up onto the sidewalk..."

"You hit the lip!" shouted Joshua.

"And flew head first into a wall?" added Toby hopefully.

"Well, almost," he admitted sheepishly. "I hit the lip and flew headfirst into a bush!"

"Oh, Dude," exclaimed Joshua in loud sympathy.

"Public biff, the worst kind," added Toby.

"Yep," agreed Mr. Monahan, "the worst kind."

"Are you hurt?" asked Chandra in her deep smoker's voice.

"A little," he admitted, "but mostly it's my ego that's bruised. Two students helped pull me out of the bush. I'll probably have them in class next year, knowing my luck," he smiled ruefully.

Tiffany laughed. She liked Mr. Monahan. He seemed like an easy person to talk to.

He went on, "Well, on to better things. Now, I made sure each of your groups has at least one member who is a student here at McQueen High School. For your group time, I want you to start by having the McQueen students give you a tour of their campus. Take about twenty minutes for this. Touring the high school will probably set the tone for remembering your most embarrassing moments. I think high school is full of embarrassing moments. You can either share your writing during this tour, if you find quiet places inside the building to talk, or you can find a place to sit outside after the tour. You know the drill. But today, you'll need more time so be back here by nine forty-five. Off with you!"

Tiffany turned toward Sam as they headed out the door, "You're our tour guide, Sammy!"

"Sammy?" Sam said in disbelief.

"Yep. It's my new nickname for you. You're more Sammy than a Sam."

"I like it!" added Tyrell as he and Orlando followed the girls up the side of the school toward the front of the building. "Sammy!" he said with feeling.

"I don't know," said Sam thoughtfully. "I've never had a nickname before. Well, I guess Sam is a nickname. It's just what I've always been called, that and a few bad names."

"Really?" said Tiffany. "Everyone in my house has a nickname. Nobody is called by their actual name."

"What do you mean?" asked Orlando. "Don't they call you Tiffany?"

"No, we all have love names. At least that's what my dad calls them. Mine is GeeGee, you know, from Min-Gee. Hanju's is JuJu. Mom is *Uma* and Dad is *Apa*. Of course, *Uma* and *Apa* are just Mom and Dad in Korean, but they still seem like love names to me."

"How did it start?" asked Sam seriously.

"I don't really know," Tiffany shrugged. "I guess when you care about someone you automatically want to give them a name that sounds comfortable to you."

At this, Sam stopped in her tracks. Tyrell and Orlando, who had been following close behind the girls, almost ran into them. Sam stared at Tiffany intently. "And you want to change my name to Sammy?"

Tiffany looked back at Sammy, understanding their relationship was on the brink of rising to a new level. She did want to give Sammy a love name. She wanted to break through the painted-on "tough girl" exterior to the soft Sammy she had seen yesterday. She wanted to get to know the real person under all that make-up. "Yeah, I do," she said honestly.

Sam stared at Tiffany a while longer her face softened. "Okay, but only if I can call you Tiff. Tiffany is way too girly a name for you!"

The boys laughed in agreement.

"That's perfect!" said Tyrell. "Tiff fits you!"

"Fine!" said Tiffany, stopping again and turning to face the boys. "Then you," she said, pushing her finger into Tyrell's chest, "will be

Ty. And you," she said pushing her finger into Orlando's chest, "will be Lando!"

"Lando," laughed Tyrell, "Perfect!"

"Shut up, Ty!" said Orlando, shoving Tyrell sideways as they walked.

Tyrell, laughing, shoved him back.

At last, they gathered at the front entrance of the school.

Sammy seemed to be enjoying her role as the tour guide. She turned to them and held up her hand gracefully, like a car model. "Well, here it is: prison, sweet prison. What do you want to see first?"

"Show us where you hang out, Sammy," said Ty.

"Okay, Ty," replied Sammy with emphasis, "right this way."

She swept forward to open the front door and trotted off into the building. The school walls outside looked brown and weathered but the inside walls were bright with freshly painted colors. They walked fast to keep up with her. Turning right at the first corridor, Sammy held her arms straight out as she continued to walk fast up the hall referring to the art lining the walls along the corridor. At the end she stopped, "And this is the art wing. And this," she said, stopping outside a door, "is where I live." She tried the door, but it was locked. Its small window was covered by a poster.

She complained, "Bummer, I can't show you the art room."

Suddenly, she collapsed onto the floor into a cross-legged sitting position. "Well, at least I can tell you my story while sitting in my happy place."

Tiff looked around her. This wall was painted orange, but art projects of watercolor and acrylic lined the walls. Several glass cases, placed between each door, contained ceramic pieces made by amateur artists.

Sammy took her blue notebook from her camo-patterned book bag. The others followed suit. They sat on the floor in a circle.

Tiff wondered if Sammy would talk more about her family and the event that she'd alluded to between her and the stepdad. *I hope she does; it would help us understand her better.*

Sammy read, "My embarrassing moment: when I was in sixth grade we moved to LA. My mom decided, for some unknown reason, I should go to Catholic school even though we weren't Catholic.

"Well, my first day I walked into my new classroom wearing this god-awful uniform. Everyone was sitting quietly reading at their desks and suddenly all of the kids stood up and crossed themselves! Then they sat down. I thought they were praying for protection from me or something! I felt really embarrassed. The teacher looked up at me and was just going to say something when suddenly this voice came over the loudspeaker. Again, all of the students stood up, turned towards me and started shouting this prayer together along with the voice on the loudspeaker. I had no idea what they were doing! It felt like a group exorcism or something. Like they'd been warned about me and were protecting themselves from a witch! I was so freaked, I started crying and ran from the room."

Tiff was shocked. This wasn't the kind of story she had anticipated coming from Sammy. It was hard to think of Sammy, dressed from head to toe in black, as a scared little girl in a Catholic uniform.

Sammy continued, "It took the teacher a long time to talk me into coming back. That was one helluva first day!" She stopped reading and looked up.

Lando was the first to speak, "But I don't get it. What were they doing?"

"I didn't get it for a while either. I found out later that they had been taught to stand up and cross themselves whenever they heard an ambulance or fire engine siren go by. They were saying a prayer for the person who might be hurt and for the fire fighters or paramedics. It just happened that I walked into the classroom for the first time as a siren went by on the street. So that's what the first crossing was about."

Tiff rolled onto her back and howled with laughter. "That's hysterical!" she said. "You thought they were praying for protection from you!" she kept laughing.

Sammy sat very still. "Well, it wasn't funny at the time."

Ty grinned at her, "But you've got to admit, it is pretty funny now."

Sammy began to smile a little. "Yeah, I guess it is when you think about it."

Lando interjected, "What was the other thing? Why were they shouting at you?"

"Oh," Sammy chuckled. "Well, as it turns out, there was a crucifix on the wall over my head. Every morning they start school by praying 'The Angelus' prayer together. It's a prayer where you stand up and face the cross when you pray it. That's what they were doing, and I was just in the way."

Tiff was on her back laughing again and Ty was trying to hold in his snickers. Lando started to laugh, so finally Sammy joined in. Then they were all laughing together. Sammy's laughs were punctuated by short snorts and that made everyone laugh harder.

Suddenly a door down the hall opened and a stern woman poked her head out of the door. "Please, I'm trying to hold a class in here. Could you take your conversation somewhere else?" She almost slammed the door.

They looked at each other in surprise, tears springing to their eyes as they tried to suppress their laughter long enough to get up and walk.

"Where's the gym?" squeaked Tiff.

Sammy said, "This way," turning back to the way they'd come. She wove in and out of hallways so quickly it was difficult for Tiff to look around as she trotted. All hallways seemed to look alike, aside from distinctive colors. Each seemed to have a theme, such as English or Geography. Tiff guessed maybe the classrooms were grouped by subjects. Her school grouped classrooms by grade level and Tiff found that she liked the theme idea better. While streaming through a blue hallway lined with lockers, she'd noticed a large paper cut-out of George Washington chatting with Abraham Lincoln and guessed they must be passing through the history wing.

They arrived at the gym to find it empty. There were no classes being held inside this summer. They sat on the basketball bleachers while Tiff told her story instead of reading from her notebook. She loved telling stories, and hearing them. Story-telling was the one thing she really enjoyed about her family get-togethers.

She got up on the gym floor and acted the story out as she spoke it. "You see, Hanju and I had the same color gym shorts. I accidently took his to school one day. He's bigger than I am, even though he's younger. So, we were playing basketball in gym and my shorts kept slipping off my hips." Tiff mimicked dribbling a ball while trying to keep her shorts up. "Then, I got so into the game that I forgot about it. The ball came to me and I did a perfect lay-up, sunk the shot and lost the shorts!"

Lando flopped on his side, laughing. Sammy grinned as she shook her head, and Ty chuckled. Tiff laughed harder than anyone. She loved to laugh out loud even though it was considered inappropriate in her home. She was enjoying herself.

"My turn," said Lando when he'd caught his breath. "Where's the cafeteria?"

Sammy headed out of the gym. To her surprise, the way out of the gym took them to an outdoor courtyard in the middle of the campus. The courtyard was lined with benches and vending machines and had doors on every side that students could use to get to and from classes. They crossed the courtyard to the cafeteria. Tiff was beginning to like this school more and more. She would love to sit down and eat lunch outside, but at her school the only thing outside was the parking lot.

Once inside the cafeteria, Tiff felt more at home. The long, white lunch tables looked the same as the ones at her school, and the room layout was similar, with a food line along a steel, self-serving section. There were also coffee stations, condiment stations, and more. They plopped down at a table. Other people from their class sat in small groups. Still other students were scattered around the room, studying and drinking coffee.

Lando opened his notebook and began to read. "My freshman year of high school, I had a crush on this girl in my math class named Vanessa. I tried to think of all these ways to get her to notice me. She worked in the cafeteria at lunch so I always stood in her line, even if I didn't want what she was serving. One day, I got up the courage to talk to her. I decided to say something funny in Spanish since I knew she had a Spanish class. Yes," he nodded sheepishly, "I had memorized her schedule. Anyway, I decided to say, 'that blue hair net brings out the color of your eyes!'"

Ty let out a moan.

"I know, it was lame, but it gets worse. Her Spanish wasn't as good as I thought and she didn't really understand what I said. She blushed really red, and it got awkward with people in the line waiting behind me. She tried to form a sentence in Spanish that said, 'I had embarrassed her,' but the word in Spanish for 'pregnant' is similar to the word in English for 'embarrassed,' so she actually said something like 'I had made her pregnant.'"

"Oh no," said Ty.

Lando continued, "So then, before I realized her mistake, I shouted, 'I didn't get you pregnant!'"

"You didn't!" said Tiff.

"Yes I did," said Lando, shaking his head. "So you can see why I never got anywhere with Vanessa. She would never talk to me again."

Sammy and Tiff started laughing and Ty shook his head, saying, "Man, you really know how to impress a girl."

"Hey," said Lando, "I'm getting better." He smiled sheepishly. "And, now we get to hear what *you* did."

Ty nodded, "Do you have a music room?"

"Sure Ty, this way." Sammy led them down another hallway to several music rooms, trying each door handle while she walked. The third one opened; the room was empty.

Ty walked in and stood by the piano bench. "Okay, this is the painful story of my first piano recital."

"What?" said Tiff. "You said you weren't musical!"

"I said that I don't 'sing.' You can't live with my mom and not play an instrument. I got stuck with the piano." He gestured to it and sat down.

"Play something," begged Lando.

"Yes, play!" said Sammy and Tiff together.

"Well, if you are good girls and boys and let me tell you my story, I just might be persuaded to play for you." The three instantly sat down and faced Ty with the rapt attention of well-behaved children. "Okay, kiddies," he played along, "it went like this:

"I practiced hard for my first piano recital. I really wanted it to be great because my mother, after all, was the piano teacher. I wanted to make her proud and practiced extra hard. The big night arrived. The auditorium was full of parents and nervous students. I was the last one to perform. I know my mom put me last because I was the best and she wanted to close the show with her pride and joy. I was playing Pachelbel's Canon in D. It's a hard piece for an eight-year old. I was dressed in my finest black pants, white shirt and black tie. I performed the piece flawlessly and then stood up next to the piano to bow. People clapped, but not as loud as I was expecting for the great performance I'd just given. In fact, some people were snickering and I was confused, thinking I'd made a mistake in the music without knowing it.

"I left the stage and on my way into the green room saw a mirror to my left. I looked. My zipper was down and my white shirt was sticking out the hole."

"Oh no!" yelled Lando, holding his head in sympathetic agony.

"Bummer," said Sammy.

"Awful!" said Tiff.

"It was. In fact, I've refused all public performances since then, recitals anyway."

"Now you have to play for us," said Lando. "You promised."

"Yes," the girls agreed.

"Okay, I'll play you my recital piece. But first, let me check my zipper!" He pretended to zip up his fly. He began to play and the whole room came alive with beautiful music. The three sat perfectly still and listened in dazed wonder.

Ty, you are just full of surprises, thought Tiff. *Looks, brains and talent! You're killing me here.*

When Ty finished, Lando started the chant, and then Tiff and Sammy joined in, "Ty! Ty! Ty! Ty!"

Ty stood up gave a slight bow and began pounding on the keys. What came out was a fast dance tune. As Ty pounded his way through the piece, Tiff could not hold still. She jumped to her feet and started dancing around the room. Then Lando joined her. Only Sammy stayed seated. Tiff bounced over to Sammy and held out her hands, but she shook her head. Tiff begged with puppy dog eyes and Sammy gave in. She took Tiff's hands and was pulled up. Tiff spun her around and let go. Soon the three were dancing wildly around the room. They were interrupted by a loud knock at the door. It took a moment for them to notice the tall, bearded man standing at the open door. Ty saw him first and his playing stopped, which caused the dancers to stop mid-move like broken dolls.

"Although you play well, young man," began the bearded man, "I'm very sure you are not supposed to be in this room unattended. I've called the custodian to come lock the door now, so you need to move along."

The man turned to Sammy, who was dancing closest to him. "Whose class are you supposed to be in?"

Sammy didn't hesitate before answering, "Mrs. Johnson's English 201; we're on a break."

"Then you'd better get back to your portable now." He held the door open for them to leave.

They filed out and headed through the front of the building into the sun, squinting until their eyes adapted to the light.

That was a blast, thought Tiff. "How did you know what teacher's name to say?" she asked Sammy.

"I remembered the two choices from the summer school schedule. Mrs. Johnson teaches in the portable next to us."

"Man, you can lie really well," said Lando admiringly.

"It's a gift," agreed Sammy, smiling. "I didn't want Mr. Monahan to get into trouble because of us."

"You did well," said Ty, fiddling with his phone. "But we still have 20 minutes!"

"Hey, let's sit up at the tennis courts," said Tiff, pointing up the slope at the side of the building where the courts had just come into view.

They headed up the slope to the courts. Heat was radiating off the blacktop at an uncomfortable temperature. "Never mind, it's too hot!" said Tiff.

"How about the grass above the soccer fields?" said Sammy, pointing to the right, downhill from the tennis courts.

"Cool beans!" agreed Tiff.

"Cool beans?" asked Lando, looking confused.

Tiff shrugged her shoulders in response. "I like words, what can I say?"

They flopped down on the grass.

Lando began, "Hey, Ty, how did it go talking to your parents about church?"

Ty's head tilted to one side and he held still.

Tiff knew by now that this meant he was thinking.

Finally, he spoke, "Pretty awful actually. There was a lot of 'as long as you live in my house, you will do what I say," he said in a high voice, imitating his mother. "But I decided before I started the conversation, I was going to keep my cool. I kept repeating whenever I got a chance, 'I will not be coming with you to church anymore.' Then Mom started to cry; she never cries."

"So is that it? Did you give in?" asked Tiff.

"Well, sort of," said Ty, picking at the grass. "The thing is, I play the piano for my sisters whenever they do special music. I told Mom she could play for them from now on and she said, 'You know I can't always be there because of my work schedule.' So I agreed that if they had special music, and Mom couldn't be there, I'd help. I'm just worried she's going to start scheduling specials and work at the same time," he smiled weakly.

"You did it, though," said Tiff. "That was brave."

"Yeah, I guess."

"So," interjected Sammy, "did your dreaming stop last night?"

"Actually, no." answered Ty. "Not only did I have the dream again, but this time I saw her face."

"The face of the girl you're supposed to rescue?" whispered Lando.

"Yeah, I was at the same place running through the trucks looking for her, and then I saw her running ahead of me. She had jean shorts and a red top on. You know the kind of top that scoops down the girl's back and ties around her neck?"

"A halter top?" asked Tiff.

"I guess." He shrugged, "She had long, blonde hair. I finally caught up to her and called her name." He paused here, looking up to the right, "Though, I don't remember it now. Then she turned around and I saw her face. She was crying."

"What did she look like?" Sammy asked, her voice, even quieter than usual, came out as a whisper..

"She had really green eyes. Big eyes, and red lips. And a small nose with a piercing in it and one of those dimples in her chin." He said squeezing his chin into a cleft.

Sammy grabbed an art pad out of her bag.

"Are you going to try to draw her?" asked Tiff.

Sammy flipped open to a page in the pad and as she turned it toward them, "I think I already did!" On the pad was a drawing of the blonde girl, exactly as Ty described her.

"That's her!" Ty shouted as he leaned toward the art pad. "Is she a friend of yours?"

"I've never seen her before," said Sammy. "I told you I don't draw anything in particular. I just draw what comes to me. This is what came to me last night."

"Are you lying?" asked Lando.

"Why would you say that?" said Sammy, turning on Lando with a high voice, ready to fight.

"No. Sorry. I didn't mean anything, it's just you just told us over there you're a good liar."

"Well, that's different," Sammy said defensively. "It was necessary to protect Mr. Monahan. I don't lie about my art."

"But, how did you draw someone I was dreaming about?" asked Ty with intensity.

"How did you dream about someone I drew?" Sammy's eyebrows drew together. "Maybe you saw my art book and something I drew triggered your dream."

"I never saw your art book, and you *said* you just drew that face last night."

"I *did* just draw this face last night."

Whoa, thought Tiff, things had gone from fun to angry so fast she felt off balance. She wanted… needed, them to be friends. She jumped in. "Hey, guys, wait. Settle down! Maybe it's a message. Maybe, you know, we're supposed to help this girl."

"A message from what, aliens?" asked Ty sarcastically. "It makes no logical sense that she comes to my dream and Sammy's art page all in the same night."

"Not everything in this world is logical," said Lando. "Why do good people die? Why do floods happen? Why do people get cancer? None of that is logical."

"Well this," said Ty, jabbing a finger toward Sammy's drawing, "doesn't make any sense. And it sure as hell isn't logical!" He jumped up, grabbed his bag, and stomped downhill to the portable. He spoke over his shoulder as he walked, "If this is some kind of a joke, I'm not amused!"

The three sat in shock, watching him walk away. Tiff didn't know if she should run after him or stay with Sammy.

"It's not my fault I drew her!" Sammy said frowning, her face tightened. She turned to Tiff and Lando shoving her art book back into her bag.

"Hey," said Tiff, grabbing her hand, "don't worry about it. He's just upset because something happened he can't explain logically. We'll work this out together, you'll see."

Sammy kept jamming things into her bag.

"Yeah," said Lando. "I, think this is totally cool! I mean, what if we are supposed to rescue this girl and we are getting more and more clues as to how?"

"Whatever," said Sammy as she stood.

"It's time to come back in," they heard Mr. Monahan yelling from the portable down below them.

Tiff and Lando picked up their stuff and started down the hill. Sammy was frozen in her tracks. For the second time that day, Tiff took her arm and coaxed her to follow.

CHAPTER TEN
THE WEEKEND

THE BLUE GROUP HAD NO TIME TO TALK until the next morning. After Mr. Monahan dismissed them, they walked up to their grassy spot. Sammy was still angry – she had even thought about not going to class. She would have stayed home if it hadn't been for the dancing the day before. She had really enjoyed the first part of their time yesterday. She loved laughing with the others and hearing their stories, and dancing. She couldn't remember the last time she had danced,and then Tiff had given her a nickname. That meant a lot to her too. Finally, she had decided to go, but she wasn't going to make it easy on Ty because he'd hurt her feelings and needed to know it.

They sat on the grass in the morning sun. No one spoke. Finally, Ty's voice broke the silence.

"I need to apologize for leaving angry yesterday." He looked up at Sammy, "Especially to you Sammy. I thought about it all night and there is no way you could know what I was dreaming."

"*That's* what I was trying to tell you," Sammy frowned, nodding.

Ty said, "I know…it's just that it doesn't make sense; it's beyond unusual. But now I understand what you were all trying to say. Just because something doesn't make sense doesn't mean it can't be true."

"And?" asked Tiff.

"And what?"

"And you didn't mean to hurt Sammy's feelings, did you?"

Ty's mouth hung open. He looked at Sammy who was sitting with her arms crossed against her chest.

"Of course, I never meant to hurt your feelings, Sammy."

"Well, you did. You implied I was lying or I knew the girl. I told you I didn't know her and yet you wouldn't believe me."

"Yeah, I was being a jerk," admitted Ty.

Sammy stared! She was used to fights that went on for hours, nobody admitting a wrong. But Ty was actually apologizing and looked embarrassed. She thought about continuing to pout, her normal way of dealing with anger. But, somehow she didn't feel that angry anymore.

"Apology accepted," said Sammy. "But there's something you need to know about me. I don't lie to friends although I will lie to protect friends."

"Are you admitting we are friends then?" asked Tiff.

Sammy looked at her and then gave a brief nod. She turned to Ty and noticed his eyes had dark circles under them.

Ty smiled and relaxed his shoulders a little. "Thanks, I was thinking about it all night. I think we need to meet outside of school so we can really look at what's happening here."

"I'm down," Tiff popped off almost before Ty finished. "When and where?"

"How about tomorrow?" suggested Sammy. "We don't have class, remember?"

"I have to work at the cleaners on Fridays," whined Tiff.

"Well, how about Saturday?" offered Ty.

"I have tennis lessons in the morning," said Tiff.

"I have to work all day," said Sammy.

"You didn't say you had a job," noticed Ty.

"Well, it's not much to speak of. I just work the front desk and sweep floors on Saturdays at the beauty shop on Kings Row. Helps pay for my bus pass and things. How about Sunday?"

Tiff shrugged, "I have church."

"You sure are busy!" said Sammy.

"That's my family's parenting philosophy," explained Tiff. "My dad says it's best to keep kids busy and broke – keeps them out of trouble!"

"Don't they pay you to work at the cleaners?" asked Ty.

"They do," said Tiff, "but not much. It coverslittle stuff like movies and music. My parents don't give us an allowance or anything. You should see the stink they make whenever I have to pay for tennis or buy uniforms and stuff. They usually cave when I remind them that sports open up scholarships for college."

"I thought they wanted you to be a doctor?" asked Lando.

"They do, but on some level they must know I need a backup plan 'cause my grades aren't going to get me any scholarships. They also keep saying sports will round out my application for Med school."

"Well, I have to work Saturday and Sunday in the summer anyway," explained Lando.

"What do you do, Lando?" asked Tiff.

"My mom's friend has a construction company. I'm too young to work there, but he lets me help with cleaning up and stuff on the weekends."

"So, what does that leave?" asked Sammy.

"Um, Friday night?" asked Tiff.

"Sorry," said Ty, "I have to play at my sister's concert."

"And I have to babysit," said Sammy.

"I thought you got out of playing piano?" Lando said, turning to Ty.

"My mom is out of town at a music teacher's conference, so that leaves only me."

"Don't you have a job?" asked Lando.

Ty looked down. "Not really, though I wish I did. My Mom says my job right now is school and there's plenty of time to work. Next year I'm hoping to work some at the tutoring center after school."

"So your parents just give you money whenever you want it?" asked Lando.

"Yeah, pretty much," said Ty, looking uncomfortable.

"Where is the concert?" asked Tiff, trying to change the subject.

"It's at Wingfield Park." Ty looked relieved to have the focus shift off his lack of work. "They're having gospel choirs from all over."

"Well, what if we all meet there?" asked Lando.

"That might work," said Ty. "Our group will go on third. There are five groups. I think we'd have time to talk either before or after."

"I guess I could bring Charity with me," said Sammy. "We could take the bus down."

"I could probably come if I tell my folks it's for school. Though they might make me bring Hanju and he won't be happy about that," offered Tiff.

"It sort of is for school," said Lando. "I can probably get there. My mom goes to work downtown at five. I could catch a ride in with her and then maybe take a bus back."

"Or, I can give you a ride home," volunteered Ty. "I can't pick anyone up 'cause I have to be there early for sound check, but I can give you all a ride home. I'll just tell my sisters I need to drive my own car that night."

"You have a car?" asked Lando with awe.

"Yep," Ty grinned sheepishly. "It was a hand-me-down from one of my sisters. It's an old Subaru Station Wagon."

"I wish I had a car. I want a sleek, dark blue Mustang convertible," said Lando, sitting up.

"Not me," said Ty, "I want a hybrid that gets good gas mileage."

"I want a Jeep, so I can go off-roading!" added Tiff. "A red Jeep!"

"Focus, folks, focus!" said Sammy. "We were making a plan."

"Oh, yeah," said Lando, deflating like an old balloon.

"Okay," said Ty. We meet downtown by the river at seven. I'll try to bring a couple blankets for us to sit on. What else should we bring?"

"What do you mean?" asked Lando.

"Well, what should we bring help us figure out what's going on? Sammy, how long have you been drawing things like this?"

"Things like what?"

"You know, things that just 'come to you.'"

"Well, I guess it's been a few years."

"Hey," said Tiff, "you drew that picture of the knight rescuing the girl from the dragon, too!"

"So?"

"Well, do you have any other drawings like that, you know, with a rescue-type theme?"

Sammy closed her eyes to think for a moment, "You know, now that you mention it, I do. I've drawn a lot of rescue themes lately."

"That's it!" said Ty. "Bring any drawings you think fit this theme. Maybe they'll give us clues about what's happening."

"Ty," said Lando, "have you had any more dreams?"

"No," said Ty. "Only the same dream last night and I'm getting sick of it. Can you imagine what it's like waking up in a cold sweat and knowing you're supposed to do something but not knowing what?"

"Sounds awful," said Tiff.

"Did you get any new information in your dream though?" asked Lando.

"Well, there was one thing," said Ty. "I sort of know her name. I call it out in the dream and then she turns to look at me, only when I wake up, I can't remember it. It's a 'D' name like Debbie, or Dawna or something. This whole thing is making me feel crazy. I feel like, if I knew her name, I'd be one step closer, ya know?"

"We'd be one step closer," corrected Tiff. "Remember, we're in this together.

CHAPTER ELEVEN
THE CONCERT

THE EVENING OF THE CONCERT WAS WARM, but Ty brought extra blankets and a warm coat because he knew the minute the sun went down, it could get chilly. He'd laid out two blankets in the back of the grass amphitheater so the group could still see and hear the concert but not bother other people when they needed to talk. People were arriving with their baskets and blankets in tow.

His family, seated down near the front of the amphitheater, was greeted warmly by most of the arrivals. Reno was a small town in many ways. In fact, its motto was "the Biggest Little City," but Reno was tiny if you were black because Reno was an overwhelmingly white town. It was impossible to fly under the radar if you were black *and* a Dupree. His family had too high of a profile for Ty's tastes. Shaundell, his oldest and most motherly sister, brought a basket of food for him and his friends. It smelled amazing.

Lando arrived first, walking up to the park from the downtown casino where his mom worked. While Ty did his sound check, Lando raided the picnic basket and had already scarfed down a full plate of chicken, coleslaw and "the most delicious brownies ever."

Afterward, he stretched out on the blanket for a nap in the fading sun.

Ty was glad Lando was independent and self-sufficient. He had lots of people to greet, and he would have felt bad leaving his friend alone on the blanket for so long, but Lando seemed content to lie in the warmth and snooze.

Tiff arrived with her sulky brother, Hanju, in tow. Hanju, although younger by a year, was already an inch or so taller than his sister.

She was much shorter than Ty had realized. *Maybe five-foot-four at the most,* he thought. *It's just that she has such a big personality; I always thought she was taller!* He realized she looked different in other ways too: she was wearing fitted jeans, instead of her sweat pants, plus a feminine white lacy top, and if he was not mistaken, she was wearing makeup.

"Hi!" yelled Tiff as she marched up the hill waving, Hanju plodding behind her. She smiled widely at her friend.

"Pretty," Ty smiled. That was the word describing Tiff tonight. When his voice echoed in his ears, he realized, too late, he'd spoken his thoughts aloud.

"What?" said Tiff, the smile dropping from her face.

"What?" questioned Ty, his voice cracking.

"Did you just say 'pretty?'" asked Tiff, her cheeks getting pink.

"Did I?" asked Ty. "I mean, I did. I mean, you do look different tonight. I mean, pretty. I mean, uh, nice." He stopped talking because he was making things worse.

"Um, thanks." Tiff mumbled – aware her brother was standing behind her watching this whole interaction with intense interest. She swung to Hanju and glared. He returned a smirk that said, *I've got something on you!*

She turned back, "Ty, this is my brother, Hanju."

Ty offered his hand and Hanju shook it. "Nice to meet you, man," said Ty. He turned, gesturing them toward the blanket where Lando was now waking up. "My sister brought food for us if you're hungry."

"Food," said Hanju, who practically dove into the basket.

"Sorry, he's hungry all the time." She shrugged, "Growth spurt I guess."

They stood together uncomfortably, watching as Lando introduced himself to Hanju and helped him find paper plates and plastic forks. "There's Sammy!" said Tiff, looking relieved. She bounced off down the hill. Sammy and her sister stood out like pale ghosts in a sea of dark faces.

Ty released a breath he didn't know he'd been holding. *Real smooth!* He watched as the three trudged up the hill together. Sammy's little sister, Charity, looked like a classic waif from a Dickens novel, with hair that stood out at odd angles and a sallow, unwashed face. When they got to Ty, Sammy said, "This is my sister, Charity."

Ty bent at the waist and smiled at Charity. He felt the need to protect her, like he'd found a little bird kicked out of the nest too early. "I'm glad you came." Charity rewarded him with a tiny smile.

The Blue Group sat down on the blankets and began to eat and talk at the same time. Hanju seemed comfortable, but Charity ate dainty bites while glancing shyly at the teenagers.

The concert started and the first choir up was Greater New Hope Baptist. They walked proudly onstage in twos from both sides until the stage was full. They swayed to music in their bright red robes. A large part of the audience near the front- left of the stage chanted, "Here come the choir! Here come the choir," and applause burst from the crowd.

Ty watched his friends enjoy the concert. It was interesting to see his world through their eyes. They sat still – awestruck with wonder at the power and majesty of the music. When the concert goers got to their feet to dance, his friends jumped up with gusto. When the choir gave a call, the audience quickly responded. Soon, Lando, Tiff and Sammy were shouting "Amens" with the best of them. Even Hanju and Charity were enjoying themselves. They were having so much fun they completely forgot about their "other" agenda.

Ty said, "That's Reverend Taylor," gesturing toward a large, dignified man on the left side near the stage, clapping to the music and smiling. "He and my Dad have been friends for a long time. His church has always had a powerful choir."

The happy group joined the rest of the crowd in hearty applause when the first choir finished. Reverend Taylor climbed up onstage and said, "Welcome everyone to a night of gospel. Our gospel choir tradition is about coming together in unity to praise God. My wife told me I couldn't preach tonight!" The crowd laughed knowingly, those front-left laughed the loudest. "So, I'll just say welcome, and enjoy! Now join me in welcoming the choir from Second Baptist Church." The crowd cheered.

The second act was smaller, and their robes a beautiful turquoise. Tiff gasped with surprise when a little girl came to the front to belt out her song with a powerful voice.

Sammy bent to Charity and whispered, "She's not much bigger than you. Could you sing like that?" Charity's eyes got big and she shook her head adamantly.

Ty leaned toward his friends, "Well, I have to go get ready. See you after." He walked down the hill towards the right side of the stage. He thought he would be nervous to have them here tonight, but instead he felt happy to be able to share his music. He disappeared and the next time they saw him he was wearing an emerald green choir robe and sitting behind an upright piano. His three sisters wore matching emerald green gowns and were standing in front of microphones. Two were tall and thin like Tyrell and one short and round. The shortest of the three stood slightly in front as the lead singer. The crowd shouted a warm welcome as the four Duprees took the stage. It was clear from the audience reaction that this ensemble was a favorite. Ty smiled at the crowd's roar.

Tiff, Sammy and Lando swayed together in anticipation. The sun had gone down and the air had become chilly. They draped a blanket over them and snuggled together for warmth. Ty pounded a loud introduction on the piano. Tiff's eyes were wide with wonder. When the three sisters began to harmonize, Sammy's eyes glistened with tears.

Lando whispered to the girls, his face full of longing, "I wish my mom and grandma could hear this; they'd love it."

When Ty's three-song set ended, the crowd clapped, yelled and whistled while his friends jumped up and down with joy.

Ty took off his robe and made his way back to the blankets, but he was not alone. His sisters came up the hill with him, plus his father. They were all curious and eager to meet Ty's new friends, so introductions were made all around. His sisters were wearing more casual clothes and huge smiles.

The group welcomed them. "That was fantastic!" declared Tiff.

"Beautiful," agreed Sammy.

"Awesome!" said Lando.

"Why, thank you," said the shortest sister, who turned out to be Shaundell, the eldest. "We're so glad you were able to come. My mother will be sad she missed meeting you. She sent her 'Hellos' to all of you. Tyrell told us about your group and how much he enjoys your class."

Charity tugged on Sammy's arm and she bent down to Charity who whispered something in her ear. Sammy turned toward Machell and Rachell and said, "Charity wants to know if you two are twins."

Machell and Rachell laughed, "We are, you're a smart little thing!" said Machell looking directly at Charity who looked down at her shoes, smiling.

The next choir was starting so the three sisters headed down to their own blanket, receiving congratulations along the way. Ty's dad, however, moved next to Sammy saying, "Mind if I join you for awhile?"

Yeah, I mind, thought Ty, realizing this would mess up their chance to talk about the dreams, but Sammy pulled out her blanket so Mr. Dupree could sit on it.

"Can I ask you a question?" Sammy asked Mr. Dupree.

"Of course," he said with a smile.

Mr. Dupree looked and sounded like an older version of Ty. He had a more filled-out frame, some grey on the temples of his short hair, and the same mellow voice.

Sammy hesitated because she didn't know how to properly address Mr. Dupree. "Well, Mr. Dupree, that is, Preacher Dupree?" she asked.

"Father Dupree," offered Lando.

"Pastor Dupree," tried Tiff. Ty smiled at this confusing beginning. He'd never considered that people wouldn't know what to call his father.

"Actually," Mr. Dupree said with a chuckle. "Technically it's Reverend Dupree. But Mr. Dupree is just fine!"

"Whew," said Sammy blowing up at her bangs. "Well, Mr. Dupree. We're doing a class project about dreams." Sammy saw Ty roll his eyes and begin to interrupt, but she pressed on. "And we were wondering what you think about dreams."

"Dreams?" Mr. Dupree asked. "What do you mean?"

"Well, what do you think dreams mean? Or a better question, are there different kinds of dreams?" Mr. Dupree tilted his head to the right and was silent, thinking. Tiff and Sammy shared a glance at this familiar gesture.

"I believe there are three different kinds of dreams," he began.

Ty knew his father was comfortable about giving an opinion.

"There are some dreams that are just left-over pastrami, you know, just the firing off of synapses!" he said with a grin. Ty nodded his head yes, glad his father agreed with his own ideas.

"Most dreams," He continued, "are things that your unconscious is trying to work out while you sleep."

"Yes!" Sammy blurted, glad he agreed with her interpretation of dreams.

"But, there is a third kind of dream that's rare. I call them God dreams."

"God dreams?" asked Tiff while watching Ty's eyes roll back again.

"Yes, God can use dreams to tell you lots of things. The Bible is full of dreams! Some are metaphors, like when Joseph received the dreams about famine in the book of Genesis. And some are prophecies, like God gave John in Revelation."

"But how do you tell which is which?" asked Sammy.

"Well, prophesies are more like visions. They seem very real to the person having them, and they have a purpose."

"A purpose?" asked Lando.

Reverend Dupree looked directly at Lando, "Yes, God wouldn't go to all the trouble of giving someone a vision if He didn't mean for him to act on it, would He?"

"I guess not," replied Lando glancing at Ty.

"Is that all you want to know? For your class, I mean," smiled Mr. Dupree.

"That helps a lot, thanks," answered Sammy.

"Good," said Mr. Dupree, getting up. "I'm going to go say 'hi' to Reverend Taylor. It was wonderful to meet you all." He smiled at each of them, then walked down the hill.

As soon as Mr. Dupree was out of earshot, Ty asked Sammy, "Why did you do that?"

"Why not?" she said defensively, "Your dad's a good resource."

"Yeah," agreed Lando, "he has some good insight into…" Stopping mid-sentence he glanced at Hanju, not sure if he should talk openly in front of him. "Ah, into our dream research," he continued in code.

"Sure he did," agreed Ty, "if you happen to believe in God!"

"Hey," said Lando, "I have an idea. What if we each take a different area to study about dreams? It's too dark to see Sammy's pictures right now. We could each study a different part this weekend and compare notes on Monday.

"Good idea," said Sammy. "Who should do what?"

"Well, you do Psychology, since you're already into that. Maybe go to the library and do searches or get books on Psychology. Ty and Tiff could split up the Bible, since they're both from religious families."

"I get the New Testament," said Tiff. "The Old Testament is too big and has too many begats."

Ty looked cranky about his assignment. He asked Lando. "What are you going to look up?"

Lando thought a minute, "I know, pop-culture – you know, movies, tv and stuff like that?"

"Oh sure," Ty said. "I get the Old Testament and you get movies!"

"Hey," he grinned, "someone's gotta do it."

"Whatever," said Ty playfully, punching Lando on the shoulder.

Lando dove at Ty and they began to wrestle.

Sammy turned to Tiff, "What is it with guys and wrestling?"

"I don't know. Guys! Cut it out! I wanna see the rest of the concert!"

CHAPTER TWELVE
WOULD YOU RATHER

MONDAY MORNING, MR. MONAHAN STARED at his classroom full of students who looked stunned and scared. It was clear they'd forgotten the assignment. "Don't panic! It's in your syllabus, remember? I told you all to read it carefully. It's no big deal, really. You've been sharing in your groups now for a full week and I bet you know more about each other than you know about most of the friends you've had since kindergarten." He noticed some nodded in agreement.

"I've spent the weekend reading your journals, and I know for a fact that you have a lot of knowledge amongst you. All I'm asking you to do is choose a subject that you feel you know about or interests your group, and present what you've learned to the class."

With a quick look around the room, he saw angry or sad faces, except for one group. The Blue Group was surprisingly happy or smug or excited? He tried to define them but couldn't. He was sure they were not upset. *I wonder what bonded the blues together?*

He said, "You'll be given this next week of group times to work on the project. All I need from you is two pages each on your subject. Cover it from different angles. Then next week we'll do the oral projects, and you will each get to share your findings."

At several students' groans, Mr. Monahan continued, trying to explain his reason for the assignment. "Listen, it's not enough to know how to write, and I wouldn't be doing you any favor if that's all I asked you to do. Written communication is important, but verbal communication is just as important. Just think if you put together a great resume and then couldn't talk at the interview. Trust me. I've sat on many hiring committees for this school. If people look good on paper, it gets them in the door, but if they tank the interview, they won't get hired."

A hand shot up in front.

"Yes, Chandra."

"Well," she began, "there's someone in my group that is shy so I'm just going to ask this for them. What if you're afraid to speak in front of the class?"

"Good question," said Mr. Monahan. "Public speaking is near the top – if not *the* top – of people's fears. How many of you would say you're afraid of speaking in public?"

About half the hands in the room went up, including Sammy's from the Blue Group.

"Well, that's about fifty/fifty, not too bad. I think this will be easier than usual because our class is small. We're already getting to know each other, and your group mates will be standing up front with you."

Many faces in the room were still grim and stressed. *Drastic times call for drastic measures,* he thought. "I'm going to teach you a game called 'Would You Rather.' I'll start with two sentences; then you raise your hand for the thing you'd rather do. For example, would you rather be stuck in an elevator or be stuck in a car on a bridge?"

He said each one a second time and students raised their hands accordingly. Sammy's hand went up quickly for the bridge.

"Good," said Mr. Monahan. "Now would you rather hold a spider in your hand or a snake? Spider or snake?"

Tiff and a few others looked undecided, putting up a hand for one option, and then the other. People on both sides of the question called out, trying to convince them to their side.

One voice from the snake side said, "Well, at least you know where the head is!"

One voice from the spider side said, "There's only one spider in Reno you have to worry about and that's the deadly black widow!"

Tiff shivered visibly, raised her hand and said, "Snake," weakly.

Mr. Monahan chuckled when he felt the room's atmosphere change from stress, to energy and fun. *That's what I love about high school students: their emotions can turn on a dime!* "Ready?" he asked when all the students had chosen a side. "Would you rather spend the night in juvenile hall or confront someone about a problem you have with them?"

He was quite surprised to see the majority of students raise their hands on the side of spending a night in juvenile hall. Only a handful of students were on the confrontation side, including Lando and Ty.

"Interesting!" said Mr. Monahan. "That's actually fascinating. I've got another question and this is the last one. Would you rather confront someone or speak in public?" Two thirds of the students raised their hands to the public speaking side. "Okay," said Mr. Monahan, waiting for them to stop talking. "It's interesting to me. More of you are afraid of confrontation than you are of public speaking. I think we've discovered a new number one fear! Did you notice how our fears are subjective, depending on what we are comparing them to? Half of you were afraid of public speaking until it was compared with confrontation, and then confrontation was the bigger fear. Both public speaking and confrontation are communication skills you will need to develop in order to survive in the workplace as well as your day-to-day lives. I'm glad you will get the opportunity to experience both in this class. If you haven't experienced it yet, your group will soon begin to experience conflict and confrontations that will need to happen if you are to go deeper with each other."

Lando, Tiff and Sammy all looked up at Ty, who turned his head away, smiling.

Mr. Monahan wrote five words on the board. As he spoke, he emphasized each word as he defined it. The words were Forming, Norming, Storming, Transforming and Adjourning. "In the small group dynamics theory, it says all small groups go through five stages as they get more and more honest or connected. When you first get together, your job is to form a group. In this class you were put into groups, but other groups form spontaneously with friends at work, or roommates at college, just to name a few examples.

"The second phase is when the group sets its norms. This can happened subconsciously or on purpose. For instance, a norm might be that your group starts and ends on time. For friends who plan parties together you might develop conflict over this norm because some members are time-conscious and others are more event-oriented. My wife, Sarah, and I had to work this one out when we got married. She's from a family that was always punctual and my family always ran late. It's one of the areas where we had to learn how to compromise. This is an example of an unspoken norm. In your groups, I gave you some spoken norms the first day. I said, 'each of you has an equal amount of time to share.' If I hadn't done that, think about who in your group would have dominated the discussions and who in your group might never have said a word."

At this, a few students pointed at their classmates and chuckled. In the Blue Group, the teasing was for Sammy and Tiff.

Mr. Monahan continued, "And this is where confrontation or 'storming' comes in. After the initial honeymoon period, a group has to start fighting if it is going to move from a quasi-community to real-community. The same is true of a marriage or a friendship. If you can't fight and move through the fight to reconciliation, you'll never have a deep relationship. It worries me a lot that so many of you are afraid of confrontation. We have to confront each other in love in order to build real and lasting community.

"So, there are two real challenges for you in this class, public speaking and confrontation. I think the confrontation part will be harder than the public speaking myself, but take some risks. I'd love for you to experience confrontation in this small and safe place so you can learn how to do it well for the rest of your lives.

"If you work through the problems and conflicts in your group and don't let them just fester or be ignored, your group will transform into a true working community. Really, it's worth it. I want you to try this and see what happens. Groups that have gone through storming and have reached transforming can be powerful and effective. Learning to manage conflict will improve your ability to write and speak and live.

He looked at the class to state his last bit of news. "Like it or not, most groups eventually dissolve or adjourn. Yours will end after this class is over. Since you are from different schools, there is little chance you will stay connected, except on Facebook." Some group members seemed down at this comment, but members of the Blue Group were downright grim. *Man, I'd like to be a fly on the wall when they meet.*

"Lots of groups are only temporary, like work teams that form to hire someone or theater troops that perform a play together. But some stay together, like families, well, most families anyway.

"Okay, now this week will be different from last week. I want you to choose together what your topic will be. This alone will jump-start your storming process." He smiled and several students smiled, enjoying the joke.

"Then start to work on your projects. You'll still have journaling assignments each night, but you won't be sharing them with each other unless you really want to. You will have the weekend, if you want to meet outside of class to plan your oral reports. Presentations will begin next week."

He returned to the whiteboard, picked up the marker and wrote a column of numbers one to four. "On your way out today, have one member of your group come up and sign up for a day next week. Be back here by ten. Now, off with you!"

As the students began to gather their things, Ty moved purposefully to the board and wrote "Blue Group" on day number one.

CHAPTER THIRTEEN
THE KNOWING

LANDO BEGAN TO TALK BEFORE THEY sat down. "That's just like us! We're all happy and dancing and then like, POW, confrontation city. I wonder if that means we get to transform now. It would be good timing 'cause we really need to work on this project."

"I doubt there's one conflict and that's it," said Ty.

"Ya, I bet you bounce back and forth between storming and transforming," agreed Tiff. "But this is so totally cool. It's exactly what Lando said we should do. We're ahead of everybody! Lando, how did you know about the assignment? Did you remember what the syllabus said? I just pulled it out this morning to re-read it, and when I saw the assignment, I was shocked because it's what you already told us to do."

"No, I hadn't read it, I just..." Lando thought, *How can I explain the feeling I had last night at the concert?* It was like a pressure in his gut. He felt a wave of heat in his head and knew, just knew! Knew they needed to start their research now. "I don't know how I knew, I just knew." He got a pat on the shoulder from Tiff, a smile from Sammy and a fist bump from Ty. "Well, let's see what we found out so far." They all began to dig in their backpacks and book bags.

As Tiff spoke, she pulled from her bag a big leather-bound Bible. It had gold edges and embossed letters on the front that said Holy Bible and in small letters near the bottom it read 'Tiffany Cho'. "Ty, I really loved the concert. I'm sorry my parents picked us up early. It didn't give our group any time to talk, but I really loved the singing."

Ty pulled a slim stack of papers from his backpack. "No problem, it was too dark to see Sammy's pictures anyway. I don't know why I didn't think of the darkness in the first place."

Sammy held her art pad and a journal-looking book in her lap. "It doesn't matter. I wouldn't have been able to concentrate with all that beautiful music going on. Besides, Lando's idea is even better, this way we'll all be involved.

"The only problem is," said Lando, holding up his empty hands. "My Internet was down all weekend, I have nothing. I think the phone bill didn't get paid again." He lowered his head, embarrassed.

"You have dial-up?" asked Ty.

"Yeah," said Lando, shrugging his shoulders.

"That sucks."

"Big time, but even worse, I walked to the library on Sunday to use the Internet there, and it was closed!"

"Budget cuts," said Tiff and Sammy simultaneously.

Lando perked up, "I did find one thing, though, while searching for cultural references about dreams. We watched a rerun on TV of this show called 'Medium'. The main character is this psychic who has dreams. But in her case, the dreams seem to be of situations from the past, not the future, and she uses the info to solve crimes. At least, that's what happened in the one episode I saw. It's not much." He paused uncertainly.

"No, Lando," said Ty. "It was your idea to give us all assignments in the first place and now we're ahead of the class. So you did your part for today already!"

Lando smiled, "Thanks."

Ty continued, "Let's go over what we do have."

Tiff chirped in, "I'll go first! Lando, you assigned me the New Testament to look for dreams because of what Ty's dad said. In Matthew, the first dream comes right away to Joseph when Mary found out she was pregnant with Jesus but Joseph didn't believe her. Then an angel came to him in a dream and told him not to be afraid to marry her. A little while later, an angel came to him again and told him to take Mary and Jesus to Egypt. That's two times when the dream came from an angel. I've got to tell you guys though, this is going to take a long time, the New Testament is long! I only got halfway through Matthew!"

Ty sat up eagerly, "Check it out." He held up a stack of printed computer paper. "I researched the Old Testament. I went on the computer and looked around. There's this Website called The Bible Society and you can type 'dreams' in the search engine and it gives you all the references to dreams."

Tiff rolled her eyes and sighed, "Are you kidding? That would be so much easier."

"It is," said Ty. "But, there are still a lot of references to dig through because they did a lot of dreaming back then. I need more time. I'm going to sort the dreams according to type, such as angel-related, prophesy-related, etc."

Sammy leaned forward. "Well, as you know, I was in charge of the psychological aspects. I went to the library after work on Saturday. I only had an hour so I checked out the two most likely books on dreams I could find." She opened her journal and read from it. "One is a psychology book. It says Sigmund Freud was the first to say dreams had literal interpretations like, you know, that anything you dreamed about that was long and pointed became a phallic symbol." She grinned a knowing smile at them.

"A what symbol?" asked Lando.

"A phallic symbol is anything that symbolizes a penis," said Sammy. It was harder to tell who blushed the most, Tiffany or Orlando.

"Anyway, later this guy, Fritz Perls said everything in your dream is actually about yourself."

"What do you mean about yourself?" asked Ty.

"Well, in the…" she glanced down at her notebook, "the Gestalt way of looking at dreams, if you dreamed of this girl, you would pretend she is actually a part of you and ask her what she needed to tell you. After you ask, the ball is in her court and you just wait for an answer. After you listen to what she – who is really you – has to say, you'll know better what to do."

The group sat silent, looking at Sammy like she was nuts. "Hey, don't shoot the messenger. I'm just telling you what the books say about dreams. That's the assignment Lando gave me!"

"No, you did good!" assured Lando. "Maybe you should try it, Ty."

Ty glowered at Lando. "You're kidding, right?"

"No, I'm not. What could the harm be?"

Ty groused, "I am not going to sit out here and talk to myself so you can all have a good laugh!"

"Okay, okay," said Lando. "It was just an idea."

"Oooooh, let's do some confrontation." said Tiff with enthusiasm.

"Nevermind," said Ty. "I want to see Sammy's pictures."

Everyone turned towards Sammy as she opened her art book,
talking fast. "I sorted through my pictures and realized I've been
drawing the same girl since about May of this year. I evaluated each
piece, looking for similarities and differences."

Wow, thought Lando, *she sounds like a teacher!* Lando studied
Sammy closely as she opened her art book to the middle section. *Is
she wearing less makeup,* he wondered. *She looks softer.*

Sammy held up the book. The first picture was of a small girl lying curled up at the bottom of a well; the girl had no distinct features.
"At first, I noticed the presence of this girl who we will call 'D.'"

Tiff gulped in air.

Ty said, "I don't think we can assume they're all the same girl."

Sammy looked at him seriously, "I think I will convince you they
are if you give me a chance." She sat up on her knees. "I can't believe I
didn't notice it before! D shows up in lots of my art. She is usually in
some kind of distress. Here she's at the bottom of a well." She flipped
the pages of her book to another picture. "This time the girl is alone
in a big forest." She flipped forward a few pages to a scene of a small
girl walking by big buildings. "There is only one picture where she
looks happy." Sammy paged forward to a sketch of D's face turned
upward, a smile on her face and a hand reaching down toward her
offering an apple. In this picture the face was clearly the same one
from Ty's dream. "But then later," she flipped forward, "she goes back
into distress." Sammy showed them a picture of the small girl figure
in the back corner of a locked bird cage.

Lando felt sick to his stomach. *What's going on here?*

Tiff interrupted Sammy, "but none of these are really rescue-themed."

"True," said Sammy. "Not until we get to our first day of class." She dug her notebook out of her backpack and showed them the familiar picture of a knight fighting off a dragon while a small girl curled up near his feet.

"And I drew this after our second day of class." She opened her art book and there again was the small figure. This time she was standing on her feet at the bottom of a well. Her back to the viewer, she was reaching up high, trying to grab two hands that were reaching down for her.

"The next time I drew her was the night Ty dreamed of her." She flipped to the page with D's face.

"Did you notice anything else?" asked Tiff.

"Well," said Sammy, who loved having an audience for her art, "I noticed that in most of the pictures she is very small against really big and scary objects. For instance: the well, forest, buildings, cage and dragon. But, then there are two pictures where it's just her face, very distinct. First, there is the one with the apple where she is smiling and the one from Ty's dream where it's like, a headshot. Those are easily identifiable as the same person, as D." She flipped back and forth between those two pictures.

Lando could see it now. It was the same girl in all these pictures. He couldn't take a breath.

"But I noticed that in most of the pictures she is passive. She is lying at the bottom of the well, in the cage and at the feet of the knight. But look, in two pictures she is moving: the one in the forest and the one by the buildings. She only seems happy in the one with the apple."

"I wonder what it all means," said Tiff. "Sammy, when you were drawing it, what did you think it meant?"

"To be honest," Sammy's head went down, "I just thought the girl was me."

The group sat quietly. Orlando wondered. *Did she really feel that small, that hurt?* Then, suddenly he was having that feeling again. There was pressure building in his gut, and a wave of heat hit him again. Suddenly he knew, "I know what it means," he declared.

"You do?" asked Tiff. "How?"

"I don't know how," answered Lando. "I just I know. These pictures tell a story. Can I see your book, Sammy?" She handed it to him. He leafed through to the first picture of the girl in the well.

"You see her here? She is somewhere where she feels alone, isolated and sad." He flipped to the forest picture. "So she decided to leave, run away maybe. Only it wasn't as great as it sounded and she got scared." He flipped forward to the girl and big buildings, "She got to a city and that was even scarier." He flipped to the girl smiling up at the hand with the apple in it. "Then someone offered to be her friend and she was happy." He flipped forward to the cage picture. "But look how that turned out – now she's in an even a worse situation than before."

The group looked stunned, breathless as Lando explained. It all made so much sense now that it was obvious. "And this," he said, turning to the page where the girl was reaching up to the hands that were reaching down into the well, "this is what we are supposed to do. At least what Ty is supposed to do – rescue her!"

"Why me?" asked Ty loudly.

Lando pointed to the picture, "Because the hands reaching down are black!"

The group was dead silent. They stared at the picture of the long, black arms reaching down into the well.

"Shikey." said Tiff and Sammy at the same time.

Ty jumped to his feet, "Let me get this straight." He paced as he spoke with a sarcastic tone. "There was this girl, living on a farm or something where they have wells. So, she falls in. Then she gets out somehow, and then she decides to run away through the forest to the city. There she met someone who pretends to be a friend but actually puts her in a bird cage. Then she fell in a well somewhere again, and I'm supposed to find her and pull her out? Is that what you guys are saying? Does it sound insane to anybody, but me?" He dropped back down on his knees.

Well, thought Lando, *when you put it that way, it does sound sort of ridiculous.*

Sammy kept her cool, "The pictures don't have to be literal. They can be symbolic."

"What do you mean exactly?" asked Ty.

"I mean, it doesn't have to literally be a well. It could be she felt she was in a dark place, she felt trapped, so she ran away. She doesn't have to be in a real bird cage, just feel imprisoned or trapped."

"That still doesn't explain how I'm supposed to find her and rescue her." He scrubbed his hands over his face. "Can't you just draw me a map or something?" He started to get up, but sat back down.

Lando wondered if Ty had wanted to walk away from them.

Sammy scowled. "Ty, I don't make up these pictures; they come to me. I can't force them one way or the other, just like you can't make yourself have those dreams."

"The dreams!" said Tiff. "We can't forget about the information in the dreams."

"What information?" asked Ty.

"Well, you said in the dreams you were running around between big trucks, right?"

"Yeah, eighteen-wheelers."

"Well, what kinds of places have lots of trucks? Maybe, like a warehouse distribution center? They have lots of trucks at that Wal-Mart warehouse east of town."

Lando jumped in, "Maybe a truck selling place, like a car lot for trucks?"

"Guys, guys, remember? The dream takes place at a truck stop!" corrected Ty.

"Oh, yeah," said Tiff. "Well then, there you have it!"

"There you have what?" asked Ty.

"That is where you have to go to rescue D, a truck stop."

Ty said, "Well, that narrows it down! Do you know how many truck stops are probably on the I-80 corridor or Highway 395, for that matter? And how am I supposed to know when this is going to happen? And even *if* I find her, am I just supposed to walk up to her and say, 'Hey *D*, I'm here to rescue you because my dream told me to?'"

"Right we need more information," said Sammy. "We hope you have more dreams to tell us more."

"Great, just what I want," interrupted Ty, "More dreams."

"And we can hope that I get more information from my art," Sammy finished.

"So, in the meantime," said Lando, "we have two assignments. One, we each have to keep researching dreams. I'll do the pop-culture angle. Ty, the Old Testament; Tiff, the New Testament; and Sammy, the psychology angle. We should start brainstorming about truck stops and why the girl could be in trouble."

"Three assignments," said Tiff. "We still have to write in our journals for class, but its good we're putting together all we're getting!"

"We'd better head back," said Ty, glancing at his phone. "But I thought of one more thing that would make our report more interesting."

"What?" Tiff wanted to know.

"We need more information, so we should each ask five people what they think about dreams," said Ty.

"Yeah," said Lando enthusiastically. "It would be like a poll of popular opinion! And it might help us with this puzzle."

"Exactly," said Ty as they headed down the hill to their portable.

Walking back, Tiff turned to Sammy, "Hey, Sammy."

"Yeah?"

"I think you're an amazing artist."

"Thanks!" she said with a shy smile.

"But Sammy, there's something else I also think you should know."

Sammy glanced up, worry lines creasing her forehead.

"You'd be a fantastic art teacher too."

Sammy drew back in surprise, "Teacher?"

"Yep!"

She exhaled thoughtfully. "Teacher" she said softly.

Lando considered Tiff's comment to Sammy as they headed down the hill. Tiff was right. Sammy would make a good teacher. Tiff been right about him, too. He couldn't stop thinking about what it would be like to be a lawyer. It was like Tiff had this way of seeing into people and finding their possibilities. He shook his head at the thought.

CHAPTER FOURTEEN
THREE ASSIGNMENTS

A FTER CLASS LANDO CAUGHT THE CITY BUS home. He walked into his house to the smell of *pupusas* cooking on the stove. His grandmother was making an early dinner. They always ate before she and his mom left for work. Lando's mouth watered. *Nothing better than Grandma's hot* pupusas *stuffed with cheese!* He could already taste the warm bread, crispy on the outside but soft inside, filled with dripping cheese or meat.

Tossing his backpack on the living room couch, he entered the kitchen to start his opinion poll with his grandmother. He walked up behind her and leaned down to kiss her soft cheek. She was so tiny, not even five feet tall, but she could keep up with the best of them at work. Lando's mom dyed his grandmother's hair so no one would question her age. She was a great employee and no one imagined she was almost seventy. She looked much younger and worked harder than women half her age. She had been such a faithful and hard worker that she'd been put in charge of the swing shift housekeeping crew at the Circus Circus Hotel. The women who worked for her highly respected her even though her English wasn't the best.

She smiled up at him and began talking in Spanish about her day. Her smile disappeared when she began talking about the landlord. The hot water had gone out in their house this morning. Now it was afternoon and he had not got it working yet. Lando knew once his grandmother got on a roll over the lazy landlord he'd be hard-pressed to change the subject. Complaining about their landlord was her favorite past-time. Lando's family moved into this duplex three years ago, but there was trouble from day one. It frustrated him, but he didn't know what to do about it.

He could hear the shower running in the bedroom his mom and grandmother shared. His mom was getting ready for work. *Is she taking a cold shower?* he wondered.

When his grandmother took a breath from her tirade, he interrupted as fast and as respectfully as he could in Spanish. Although Lando was bi-lingual, his Spanish was not fluent and there was no way he could speak as fast as she did.

"*Abuelita*," he began using his pet name for his grandmother, which meant 'little grandma,' "I have a question for you about a project in school."

"For school?" she repeated with the kind of happy amazement she always expressed when he spoke of school. Lando knew that because she was from a poor family, she had not attended school past the seventh grade. Orlando thought, *that's the reason she praises my scholastic abilities. She's sure I'll go to college and be the first person in the family to get a degree.*

She put the *pupusas* in the warm oven and turned to Lando. Taking his hand, she led him into the small living room, chattering on about how tall he was growing and how mature he seemed lately. When she sat down on the couch, Lando grabbed his backpack and took out notebook and pen. When he turned to face her, he was again amazed her feet did not even reach the floor. *If you didn't know her, you'd underestimate her.*

"Yes, Abuelita, my group is doing a project on dreams. I was wondering what you thought about dreams. Do you believe dreams mean anything special?"

She thought silently for a long time. Then she leaned forward, starting to speak so fast that Lando had to write as quickly as he could to keep up with her.

"Of course, dreams mean something. There are many, many stories of saints who had visitation from the Virgin Mary in their dreams and she would tell them something they must do."

"Did you ever have that kind of a dream, Abuelita?" Lando asked.

"No, no," she said shaking her head. "But in our village, when I was about eleven, I had a friend named Cecilia, and she had one of these dreams about the Lady of Peace."

Lando knew the Lady of Peace was the patron saint of El Salvador. In the 1680's a woodcarving of the Virgin Mary mysteriously washed up on the beaches of El Salvador. People attributed many miracles to her. Lando knew this because every November 21st was her celebration day in El Salvador, and his grandmother told him about it every year and made special cakes and sweets to celebrate. Even though his family had left Catholicism because of the role the priests played in the war, there were still many aspects of it that were a part of their culture.

She continued, "The lady came to Cecilia and told her that she must not go to school that day. Of course, her parents thought she was just trying to get out of school and they tried to force her to go, but she refused! That day, her father was working in the field and her mother walked into town to sell her vegetables – she grew the most beautiful vegetables! Cecilia went out into the field to take lunch to her father and found him lying in the dirt. He had a heart attack. She ran to the farm next door for help and the men carried him to a truck and took him to the doctor. If the Lady of Peace did not warn Cecilia to stay home from school, her father would have died that day."

Lando heard a sound behind him and turned to see his mother coming from the bedroom. "What are you two talking about so seriously?" she asked.

Lando considered his mother as she stood leaning against the door frame. She was taller than his grandmother, but not by much. Even though she was only forty-five, she looked much older – having worked so hard since she was young. Facing so much tragedy seemed to have sucked life from her body. She favored her father's side of the family, the more indigenous looking people of El Salvador. She did not have the fair skin of those from the more Spanish influence like her mother. Her skin was dark and her face was round and her body was square. *Like mine,* he realized and the thought made him feel a sense of pride. This was a slightly counter-cultural feeling. In his country as in many others, the lighter the skin, the more highly regarded the person. He had heard endless stories from his mother of being mistreated because her skin was dark. She did not usually let these incidents get her down though sometimes he heard her telling his grandmother about them and, on rare occasions, he heard her cry. But his mother and grandmother were two of the strongest women he had ever known.

His mother dropped out of high school because of the civil war. When they came to America, she started out as a maid at the Circus

Circus Hotel. Now she was in charge of scheduling the cleaning services for the whole place. He was proud to have come from such a strong lineage. When he had turned thirteen, his mother had moved him out of her room and moved his Grandmother in. This left him with his own room, where he could study in private. He felt their great sacrifice and love for him every day and was determined not to disappoint either of them.

"Orlando has an assignment from school!" His Grandmother said, glowing up at him.

"Can I ask you my question, too, Mama?" he asked.

"Of course, but let's do it over dinner. We have to leave by three."

Lando's mother didn't have any great stories about visions of virgins. She had a more western view of the world than his grandmother.

"Dreams," she began matter-of-factly, "are a person's way of working out their problems while they sleep. I will often go to bed with a problem and when I wake up, I know the solution. My mind works on it while I'm asleep, helping me figure it out." Lando's mother was practical.

Lando was satisfied with his first two interviews, but where would he get three more? He pondered this as his mother and grandmother kissed him goodbye and went to work. *Oh well,* he thought heading for the TV, *time to explore some pop-culture.*

WHEN TY GOT HOME THAT NIGHT, he went straight to the computer. At dinner he brought up his dream assignment. After he explained, his family launched into a lively discussion about dreams. One thing you could always count on at the Dupree's was loud and lively talk around the dinner table. No topic was off limits at his house and everyone was allowed an opinion. And unless you were announcing you'd decided to stop attending church, your opinion was usually respected.

His mother was shaped like his older and rounder sister, Shaundell. He and his Mom were the only two quiet ones in the family. They had to work harder than the others at being heard and often chose just to listen. Make no mistake about it, however, Mrs. Dupree was queen of her castle and, introvert or not, she spoke her mind. She effortlessly kept a tight rein on her strong-willed children.

His father repeated his three kinds of dreams argument he'd shared at the concert, which he now summarized as "Salami, Symbolism, and Spirit." Tyrell wondered how ministers could magically find three words that started with the same letter to summarize any subject. He could probably alliterate a grocery list!

His oldest sister, Shaundell, was a senior majoring in Sociology at the University of Nevada. All three sisters had chosen to attend UNR instead of their parents' alma-mater, Brown. Shaundell was quick to share historical information from her African-American Literature class.

"I read a research paper that stated whites believe more in predictive dreams than us, but the statistics show African-Americans *primarily* associate dreams with predictive qualities. Even more than the white population does. It said that this predictive understanding of dreams is spiritual in nature, as Dad just said. We are actually better at applying interpretive skills to dreams than whites are."

Ty found this fascinating, but then his sister Machell jumped in. Machell was a Psychology major and liked the Freudian point of view Sam told them about. She said, "I believe each part of a dream is a symbol that means something specific." This led to a long and rather hysterical, twin-talk session between Machell and Rachell. His family had coined the phrase "twin-talk" when the girls were about three. They would often talk in a way that involved finishing each other's sentences. Since Rachell was the "funny twin," and Machell the "serious twin," it came out like a comedy routine with Rachell as comedian, and Machell an unwitting straight man. Over the years, they developed twin-talk to high entertainment and could have taken their show on the road.

Tonight Rachell challenged Machell to use her Freudian techniques to interpret her recent dream. The dream was about Rachell trying on a red dress at a store only to have Machell come up and take the dress away from her. The girls were only sophomores in college so Machell had not gotten far in Psychology. She did her best to interpret Rachell's dream. She threw around words like "repression" and "phobia" while Rachell insisted the dream was simply about Machell always stealing her clothes and being jealous of her better figure. Ty laughed out loud because they were identical twins and had identical figures.

Then Ty's mom told them "You've babbled quite enough for one evening. Go do the chores and homework." All-in-all, it was quite a fun evening – although Ty worried it hadn't helped his research.

AT THE CHO HOUSE, TIFF KNEW BETTER than to bring up dreams over dinner. She knew asking her family one at a time was the best way to get answers while avoiding arguments. She started with Hanju, who was playing with his Wii and not interested in talking. Frustrated, she looked for her grandmother ,who was sitting at the kitchen table breaking the tails off bean sprouts for soup. Tiff sat down and took a sprout out of the bowl to nibble on; she felt close to her grandmother

"*Halmoni*, I have an assignment for school. May I ask you a question?" Tiff spoke in a combination of English and Korean because she understood Korean but her vocabulary was about a third-grade level. Her grandmother's Korean was fluent but she had a limited English vocabulary, so they managed conversations with some of each.

"What is it?"

"We are supposed to ask five people one question. The question is, "What do you think about dreams, and do dreams mean anything special?"

Her grandmother's eyes closed while she thought about it. "We believe no child can be born into this world without a dream forecasting their birth. The dream tells you if you were pregnant, the sex of the baby, and sometimes you learn something about the character of the baby."

"Wow," said Tiff, "I never knew that. Did you have a dream like that about Dad, Halmoni?"

"I did. My dream told me he would be a boy, and that he would be a hard worker and it told me to get him out of the Korea so he could realize his potential."

"Really! And did Mom have any dreams about Hanju and me?"

"No," she said firmly. "People in America don't know how to dream anymore. Their minds are too full of other things." Then she looked more closely at Tiff.

"Min-Gee," she said seriously, using Tiff's Korean name, "have you had a dream like this?"

Tiff looked at her grandmother, confused. Was her grandmother asking if she had a pregnancy dream? "No! No Halmoni, I haven't. Not at all! I just had to ask because this is our class assignment, that's all."

Tiff's grandmother lowered her voice. "Gee-Gee, you have changed a lot recently. It's like you are turning into a different person, so happy and positive, like a woman in love," she nodded knowingly. "You know you can talk to me if you ever need to."

"Thanks, Halmoni, really, but I'm fine. Uh, I'd better go start on my homework." She got up and left the room as quickly as she could. *Whoa, that was scary. Maybe I need to be more careful about what I ask Halmoni!*

SAMMY HAD THE SHORTEST DISTANCE to go after school. She lived just up the hill from McQueen in a large apartment complex. She stopped on the way to pick up her little sister, Charity, at the neighbor's house. The neighbor, Mrs. Anderson, babysat Charity in the morning when Mom went to work and while Sammy went to school. As soon as Sammy rang the doorbell, she could hear Charity yelling, "Am! Am!"

Am, was the name Charity had given Sammy when she was two. Charity had suffered a lot of ear infections when she was a baby and it affected her hearing. The doctor said she could not hear the "s" sound because it was so high-pitched. Consequently, she said a lot of words without an *s*, like *hock* instead of *sock* or *ister* instead of *sister*. One day Charity had surgery to put tubes in her ears. When she came out of the recovery room Sammy held her in her lap and said, "Say SSSam."

"SSSam," echoed Charity. But even though she could now say her *s* sound, she still liked to call Sammy, Am. *Hey,* Sammy realized for the first time, *I do have a love name!*

They held hands as they crossed the street to their apartment building and climbed stairs to the second floor. "How was your day?" Sammy asked.

"Mrs. Anderson watched TV all day, but I got to play with the new kittens. I'm gonna ask Mama if we can have one when they are old enough."

Sammy felt the glow of love fill her when she looked down at Charity's eager face. *She is so innocent and unspoiled. I want to keep her that way forever.*

She wondered if she had been as carefree and happy as Charity when she was seven. Unlocking the door, she led Charity into their dark apartment, which smelled like smoke from their stepdad's cigarette habit. Tossing her book bag into a basket near the door, Sammy immediately opened the curtains and windows to let in the light and fresh air. Wherever she went, Charity followed her like a shadow. Normally this would irritate her, but today she enjoyed Charity's wanting to be close to her.

"What do you want for lunch?" Sammy asked although she knew the answer. "Mac and cheese!"

"Don't you ever get tired of mac and cheese?"

"Nope."

"Hey, Chair," smiled Sammy – trying out a love name on her sister for the first time – "after lunch, will you go with me to the library so we can do some schoolwork?"

"What did you call me?" Charity's hands were planted firmly on her tiny hips and her face looked stern.

"Well, I thought you should have a nickname because everyone in my school group has a nickname. They call me Sammy and we call Tyrell, Ty and Tiffany, Tiff and Orlando, Lando. So, I thought maybe you should have a nickname too, like Chair – short for Charity."

"Can't you think of a better name than Chair?" asked Charity, sticking her tongue out through the space where her two front teeth should be.

"Well, I could call you Ity," suggested Sammy with a grin.

"No," said Charity, shaking her head.

"How about Ity-bitty Charity?" Sam began to tickle her arms.

"Okay," she said giggling.

"Okay, Ity-bitty Charity, let's go make lunch." Sammy headed into the kitchen. This apartment was the biggest one she'd ever lived in. They each had their own bedrooms and the kitchen was actually a nice size.

"You make lunch, I gotta peeeee," yelled Charity trailing off the word while she ran down the hall into the bathroom.

Sammy smiled, shaking her head. *What a kid! I think I was that carefree once, before...* she shook the rest of the bad thoughts out of her head and got out a big pot to boil water. *But Charity is having a different life than me. She's only had to move a few times so far and she was probably too young to remember the first ones. Dirk treats her like she's his own kid. And Dirk, though he's a jerk to me at least works most of the time, and helps keep food on the table. Maybe Charity has a chance to be a normal kid, with a normal life.* This thought made her smile.

As Sammy and Charity ate their lunch, Charity asked, "Can I get books at the library?"

"Yes,if you are done with the others we got last time, we can take them back and get more."

"What do you have to study?"

"I'm learning about dreams."

Charity got a funny look on her face, forehead wrinkling and mouth pursed, thoughtfully, "I had a bad dream last night. It was scary."

"What was it about?" asked Sammy, who was used to Charity having bad dreams. They had shared a room until they moved into this apartment and Sammy had often awakened to the sound of Charity crying out in the night. Sometimes she could still hear Charity crying and her mother getting up to soothe her back to sleep.

Charity even has a different Mom than I did, realized Sammy. In reality they had the same mom. But since "the incident" when Sammy and Charity had been moved out by social services, and her mom had to work really hard to get them back, she'd changed a lot. She stayed single for a while and stayed away from bars. She had more energy for paying attention to Charity than she'd had for Sammy when she was little. *I'm not jealous, but I think I'm thankful.*

"Am," said Charity, "are you listening to me?" Sammy hadn't realized that she'd stopped listening to Charity tell the story of her bad dream.

"I'm sorry, Ity-bitty Charity. What were you saying?"

"I said in the dream there was a girl running through these big trucks and she was scared and she kept saying 'Help! Help!'"

Charity had Sammy's full attention now. She tried to keep her voice even so as not to scare Charity. "What did this girl look like?"

"She had long blonde hair and a red top."

Sammy got up and retrieved her book bag from the basket, pulling out her art book and opening it to the picture she had drawn of D's face. She handed the pad to Charity.

"That's the girl from my dream!" said Charity. "Did you dream about her too?"

"Something like that," agreed Sammy, breathing slowly to calm herself.

"Is she going to be alright?"

"I think so. What else happened in your dream?"

"Nothing, I woke up after the man caught her."

"There was a man in your dream?" asked Sammy, trying not to sound too interested.

"Yep, a scary man with red hair and a bushy beard – I didn't like him. He grabbed that girl and put her in a white van. Then I woke up and called for Mom. I was scared. Are you sure she'll be OK?"

"I'm sure of it," said Sammy, with more certainty than she felt.

CHAPTER FIFTEEN
LOT-LIZARD

WHEN SAMMY AND CHARITY GOT HOME from the library, they knew their stepdad, Dirk, was there too because his Harley was parked by the curb. He was sitting in front of the TV, watching sports and drinking beer.

Predictable, thought Sammy. Dirk was an okay guy. He was good to their mom and Charity, but he treated Sammy like she was invisible in their home. Charity had only been three when Dirk and Sammy's mom started dating. He became really attached to her and seemed to enjoy playing the father figure. But Sammy was already an angry twelve-year-old by the time Dirk arrived. She'd hit adolescence early, and Dirk didn't know how to react to her moody behavior. He merely tolerated her, and they had come to an unspoken agreement to interact as little as possible.

Sammy knew Dirk had once worked as a truck driver, so she waited for a commercial break and ventured to ask a question.

"Dirk?"

He pushed mute on the remote and looked up at Sammy, "Yeah?"

"I'm doing some research for a school report and I was wondering if I could ask you a question?"

"Sure," he said, glancing back at the TV, "but make it fast."

Sammy tried to not get angry. *Isn't a person more important than a baseball game?* "I'm wondering what you know about truck stops."

"What kind of question is that?"

Sammy took another deep breath and tried again, "I'm wondering about truck stop safety," she began. "You were a truck driver; is there any kind of trouble a girl my age could get into at a truck stop?"

At this Dirk sat up and turned toward her completely. His voice sounded angry. "I'd better not hear that you're hanging around any truck stops!"

Sammy was surprised by his tone. She had expected indifference or irritation but not anger. "Of course I don't. It's just for a report I'm doing for school. Why? Is there something bad about truck stops?"

Dirk rolled his eyes as he turned back toward the game, "Is there something bad about truck stops?" he repeated sarcastically. "Look, the only girls your age that hang out in truck stops are lot-lizards, so you'd better stay far away from them," he un-muted the game to dismiss her.

Sammy knew she should walk away, but she had to know. "What's a lot-lizard?" She had a creepy feeling she wouldn't like the answer.

"Prostitutes," said Dirk, not looking at her. "Truck-stop prostitutes; they climb right up there in the truck-cage and do it with the truckers, most of 'em on drugs."

"The 'Cage,'" she felt as if she'd been kicked in the stomach.

CHAPTER SIXTEEN
CLARITY

THE NEXT MORNING, SAMMY KNEW what she needed to do. She spent half the night trying to understand the new information about the girl they were trying to help. Now she knew the girl that both Ty and Charity dreamed about might be a prostitute. She'd dismissed the idea completely at first, but it kept coming back to her in Dirk's disgusted tone, "truck-stop prostitutes." Could it be true? Was the girl a prostitute? This question kept Sammy up most of the night. She'd been thinking of D as a girl just like her, someone young, lost and hurting. The word *prostitute* brought up a whole different set of frightening images.

WHEN SAMMY FINALLY FELL ASLEEP, she dreamt of darker things. She felt hands grabbing her. She tried to run but couldn't move, tried to scream but had no voice. She woke up more tired than before she went to bed, yet now she knew for sure what she had to do.

Sammy felt Mr. Monahan was the only adult she knew who could answer her question. She planned to wait until he dismissed them to their groups and ask him if he knew anything about "lot-lizards." In her three years of high school – maybe in her entire school life – Sammy had never initiated a conversation with a teacher. Except with her art teacher, which was different; she was more like a friend to Sammy than a teacher. She was not excited about talking to Mr. Monahan, and her stomach hurt by the time she got to school. It didn't help that her group members were chatty this morning. It was hard to dodge the questions as they filed in.

"Are you sick, Sammy? You look awful." Tiff whispered , a look of concern in her eyes, as soon as they'd sat down.

"No, I'm okay, just tired." She hoped to stop the questions.

"You guys find out anything new?" asked Lando.

Sammy avoided his eyes and question by digging through her bookbag for a pen.

Thankfully, Mr. Monahan called the class to order and she relaxed. After a brief introduction, he dismissed them to go outside for their group time. She hung back. Tiff was waiting nearby as Sammy dug around in her bookbag one more time. Noticing Tiff, she said, "Go ahead, I'll catch up." Tiff shrugged and joined Lando and Ty who were waiting for them by the door.

It seemed everyone had a question for Mr. Monahan today. She watched as person after person approached his desk with questions about their oral reports. *Why does he have to be so dammed approachable?* Her initial impression of Mr. Monahan had radically changed. He was actually who he said he was, not some wannabe teenager. He rode a longboard because he cared about the environment, not because he was trying to be Mr. Cool. Finally, everyone shuffled out of the room and Sammy edged shyly up to his desk.

"Sammy," Mr. Monahan said in surprise as he noticed he was not alone. "What can I do for you today?" He smiled, and she felt encouraged to go on.

Sammy had rehearsed what she would say on her way to school. She knew lying must be be done with confidence or it wasn't believable. She inhaled and began, "I wanted to know if you've ever heard of something I learned about yesterday."

"Okay," He looked surprised but interested.

"I was at the library, working on our project and I saw an article in a magazine that was talking about girls my age getting involved in truck-stop prostitution. Have you ever heard of such a thing?"

He looked out the window as if trying to decide the why of her question. "That sounds like an interesting article. I'd like to see it."

Sammy had prepared herself for this possibility. "Well, I didn't get to read it entirely. It was lying open on a desk and then someone came and took it. I guess they were using it for a project. So I didn't see the name of the magazine or much about the article."

Mr. Monahan looked at her more closely. He sat still. Did he think she was like a wild animal that would run away if he made too much noise? "Well, actually, I have heard it, Sam. I'm curious about why you're so interested in it?"

She desperately hoped her answer would be enough for him, "I've just never heard of such a thing. It sounded so awful that I was wondering if it was really true."

"Well I don't know much, but I'll tell you what I do know. Have you ever heard of sex trafficking?"

"No," she answered honestly.

"In other countries, like, say, Thailand for instance, young girls are sometimes sold by their parents. Or sometimes they are kidnapped from home and sold into sex slavery."

"Oh."

"You see, girls your age aren't prostitutes because it is never their idea to sell themselves. They are taken advantage of by someone older and stronger. It's actually a federal crime to sell children for sex. This kind of sex trafficking is more prevalent than any of us would like to admit."

He was watching her carefully. "Are you okay? You look a little pale."

Sammy swallowed and tried to breathe through her nose. She had to get all the information he had. She needed to stay standing there and not give in to the urge to run from the room.

"I'm fine," she said while knowing she wasn't. "What does sex trafficking have to do with truck-stop prostitution?" She tried to appear only mildly interested.

"Unfortunately, sex trafficking is not restricted to other countries. I've read that in America, some young girls who have been kidnapped are sold to truck drivers for sex." He was watching closely for her reaction.

Sam blinked rapidly. He continued hesitantly, "Of course, there are also truck stop prostitutes that are there because they want to be. Just as there are many prostitutes in Nevada, both legal and illegal. But for children and teens, it's never something they go into willingly."

"Oh, well, thanks," Sammy said weakly and turned to leave.

"Sam," Mr. Monahan's voice stopped her. "If there is anything you need, anything that's bothering you, I'll be glad to help."

"Thanks," said Sammy, glancing over her shoulder. She knew from the worried look in his eyes that he meant it. "But I'm fine," She hurried out of the room.

Trudging up the hill, she finally arrived at her group's spot on the grass. They were waiting for her impatiently. "What gives?" asked Ty. "We have a lot to cover today."

"Yeah, sorry," Sammy sunk onto the grass slowly.

"What's wrong, Sammy?" asked Tiff. "I'm really worried about you."

"Well...I think I know what happened to our girl D."

"Dawna," said Ty. I definitely heard Dawna in the dream last night."

Sammy really saw Ty for the first time that day. His eyes had dark circles and his hair was less perfect than usual. *What is this doing to him?* It was bad enough on her, and now they had a name.

"What do you think happened to her?" asked Ty.

"How do you know what happened?" asked Tiff.

"Did you draw another picture?" asked Lando.

She sat there quietly until they became quiet. "I think she was sold into sexual slavery at a truck-stop."

"What?" the Blue Group shouted as one. As if a bomb had been dropped in the middle of the grass, Ty, Lando and Tiff were all shouting and asking questions at once.

"What do you mean?" asked Ty.

"How can it be?" said Tiff.

"How do you know?" asked Lando.

"Wait," said Sammy, holding up her hand to ward off the questions. "Settle down and I'll tell you why I think it's true."

When Sammy finished telling her story, the group sat in stunned silence. She thought they looked as devastated by the news as she was. They had all grown fond of D, or Dawna, as they now knew her. It was as if she was a friend of theirs, the fifth member of their group, and now she was in much greater danger then they had ever imagined.

Finally, Ty broke the silence, "Truthfully," he began.

Sammy realized she was bracing herself, waiting for Ty to call her a liar.

"It makes sense," he nodded. Sammy let out a breath.

He went on, "Think about our scenario. A small-town girl decides to run away to the big city. Someone befriends her and it turns out she's fallen into an even worse situation. The thought of it makes me sick!" he finished with a scowl.

"We should tell the police!" said Tiff.

The group grew silent. Sammy pictured how well that would work as they made a report about a girl in danger they'd never met, but only dreamed about. She pictured and discarded the idea; apparently, so had Tiff.

"Never mind," Tiff said, defeated.

"Maybe we could tell Mr. Monahan?" ventured Sammy. She remembered his concern and the way he offered to help.

"He'd never believe us," said Ty. "And we still don't have enough information to do anything about it."

"Oh, I forgot to tell you about Charity's dream!" said Sammy excitedly. She recounted the lunch-time discussion with her little sister.

"Are you kidding me?" said Lando, shaking his head. "This just gets more and more weird."

"Amazing," agreed Tiff.

"Poor Charity," said Ty. "I know what it was like to have these kinds of dreams. I have trouble with them as a sixteen-year-old and poor Charity is only seven." He fell silent again. "Look guys, I think we're gonna need to meet outside of school. There's just too much to discuss in the short time Mr. Monahan gives us. When can we meet?"

They compared their schedules for the second time and agreed Saturday afternoon was the only time available for all of them to meet. Some would have to leave work early to make it happen.

"Okay, Saturday at one at the Northwest Library, right?" asked Ty as they prepared to head back to class. "I'll bring Lando and we'll meet you girls there."

"Right," they agreed and headed down the hill.

CHAPTER SEVENTEEN
The Other Sammy

Tiff's father was not excited to drop her off at a strip mall in a less familiar part of town. She assured him for the millionth time that their group was meeting for a school project. She stressed this project was due Monday. This, and the knowledge that the Northwest Library was only a few blocks' walking distance away, eventually won him over. Besides, the strip mall contained one of the few Asian bakery/markets in town and he had a list of items to pick up for his mother.

Tiff jumped out of the car in front of Casual Coiffeur's beauty salon where Sammy would be getting off work early. Pausing at the door of the salon, Tiff waved goodbye as her dad drove to the far end of the parking lot to the bakery. Chemical smells irritated her nose when she opened the door to the air-conditioned salon. After a hard tennis practice, the cool air felt like heaven on Tiff's sweaty skin. She glanced around the room, looking past the receptionist desk where a pretty girl was scheduling clients, to the busy floor of beauticians snipping and coloring hair. A sudden realization hit her. The voice of the receptionist was familiar. She looked back at the pretty girl and realized that it was Sammy. Her hair was held back by barrettes, she was without the Goth makeup and she was wearing – could it be – a dress?

Sammy glanced at Tiff but continued to talk on the phone. She offered a shy smile to Tiff's open-mouthed stare.

"Wow!" Tiff mouthed. Sammy rolled her eyes and turned her head away. *She looks great.*

Sammy was wearing a short black skirt with red leggings that came to her ankles and black ballet shoes. She had on a yellow tank top with a sheer, lacey-white long-sleeved top underneath. She looked like an anime character with bangs swept across her face. Her hair was ratted up in back and she had on dramatic eye makeup.

She looks cute! What will the guys think of this, Tiff wondered as Sammy hung up and turned to tell her boss she was leaving. Reaching under the reception desk, Sammy grabbed her bookbag and headed toward Tiff at the front door.

"What?" she asked, at Tiff's inability to stop staring.

"Uh, you look amazing."

"Oh, thanks, they won't let me dress the way I like to here, you know. I might scare away the clients and all that. But I do get my hair cut and colored for free."

"Well, you look so, I don't know, just different."

"Different?" asked Sammy sounding worried.

"In a good way," Tiff assured. "You look cool."

"Thanks, Tiff. You look really… sweaty." Sammy grinned.

"Thanks a lot!" Tiff banged into Sammy's side and was casually bumped back.

"I just got done playing tennis. I can't help it!"

"But you look fine."

Tiff looked at her reflection in the shop's outside window. Her hair was falling out of its sporty pony tail and she had on an old tank top, shorts, and dirty flip flops. *Guess I should have brought a change of clothes.* She took her hair out of the hair tie and straightened it with her fingers. It refused to lie flat because of an awkward crimp from the ponytail. Realizing this was a lost cause, she tied it back up.

"At least I got to take off my tennis shoes. Maybe I'll cool off by the time we get to the library. Tiff glanced at the bakery and saw her dad's car was still parked outside. "Hey, we're in luck. My dad's still there. Let's go see if he'll give us a ride."

They entered the shop just as Tiff's dad stepped in line to check out. Tiff introduced her father to Sammy, feeling relieved that she looked less drastic than normal. "Hi, Dad, this is Sammy from my class. Sammy, this is my dad, Mr. Cho."

"Nice to meet you, Mr. Cho," she used her best receptionist smile. *She can be charming when she wants,* thought Tiff.

"Nice to meet you, too," said Mr. Cho. Then he turned to Tiff, "Would you two like anything from the bakery?"

"May we have a ride up to the library when you're done?"

"Of course," he replied, looking relieved.

Tiff wondered if her father, who was normally a seek-and-destroy type shopper, had dawdled in the store in hopes of giving them a ride to the library. She looked at the menu to the right of her father where a woman was making tapioca teas. "May we have some bubble tea?" she asked her father.

"Of course," said Mr. Cho. "You go order and I'll be over to pay once I get my groceries."

Tiff grabbed Sammy's hand and pulled her up to the bubble tea counter.

Sammy frowned. "What's bubble tea?"

"Oh my gosh, have you never had bubble tea?"

"To be honest, I never even noticed this store."

"Well, prepare to have your life changed forever! Bubble tea is made with tapioca balls. You drink it through a big straw. You can even get it in different flavors. Do you like Mango? Mango's my favorite."

"Sure, I guess so." Sammy looked uncertain about drinking the clear balls she could see in the big pot.

Tiff turned to the lady behind the counter and ordered two mango bubble teas. Sammy leaned over the counter to watch as the lady took a ladle and dipped it into a large pot. She scooped up clear, round tapioca balls and added them to the iced fruit tea and milk drink.

Tiff's father paid the cashier as Sammy was handed her drink. "Thank you, Mr. Cho." She cautiously took a sip of tea.

Tiff watched her closely for a response. Sammy chewed the tapioca tentatively.

Tiff couldn't wait. "Well, what do you think?"

"Um, I like the tea, but I'm not used to having to chew my liquids."

Tiff and her father laughed. "You crack me up!" said Tiff. "Chew my liquids!" They headed out of the store into Mr. Cho's air-conditioned Nissan Infinity. Sammy slid into the leather back seat and Tiff turned to watch her expression as the car started talking.

"Destination?" the car asked in a robotic version of Mr. Cho's own voice. Sammy's face was priceless.

"Northwest Library," Mr. Cho commanded. Sammy looked over the seats to the dash board. It looked like the inside of a fighter jet with all the complicated digital readouts and knobs. It showed the way out of the parking lot and up to the library two blocks away. "Wow," she mouthed to Tiff.

"IF YOU BOYS DON'T STOP STARING, we won't get any work done today," teased Tiffany with a big smile. Both boys quickly looked down. Sammy was summarizing her findings on dreams according to psychology, but the boys were having trouble concentrating.

"Sorry," said Lando to Sammy. They were at a large library desk with papers spread out all around them but were unable to move past Sammy's new look.

"Sammy," said Lando, directly looking her in the eyes. "You have a nice face and you should show it off more often."

Tiff watched Sammy's response. She seemed to accept it. For some reason, Lando could say things in a neutral way that did not make people feel self-conscious.

"Thank you, maybe I'll give it a try. Now can we *please* get to work?"

"I'll go next," said Ty. He picked up his stack of Internet references. "In the Old Testament, dreams were most often associated with prophets. The prophets would interpret dreams that 'God'"- he emphasized, using his fingers to make air quotes - "had given to people. Or sometimes they themselves had dreams. The two biggest dreamers or interpreters seemed to be Joseph and Daniel. Joseph was sold into slavery in Egypt by his jealous brothers and spent a lot of time in jail. Eventually, he became a big wig in the Pharaoh's court because the Pharaoh had significant dreams. No one in his court could interpret them except Joseph.

Daniel, also working as a slave, interpreted dreams for the King. To summarize, dreams seemed to come from 'God' as a way to help people with special problems." He looked at the group. "There are lots of specific examples but that's the gist of it."

Tiff jumped in, "I'll go next. The New Testament doesn't have as much to say about dreams as I thought. Like I said before, they were usually connected to angels who came in dreams to give warnings etc."

Tiff was really excited about what else she had found and wondered if her group would find it just amazing. Pausing for effect, she began, "but I did find one reference I thought was really interesting." She looked down at her papers. "It's in the book of Acts, early in the new Christian church days. It's after Jesus left and the Holy Spirit came. This guy Peter gets up to talk and he quotes an Old Testament reference from Joel."

It says, 'In the last days, God says, I will pour out my Spirit on all people. Your sons and daughters will prophesy, your young men will see visions, your old men will dream dreams." She looked up at them, hopefully.

"I have that 'Joel reference,' too," Ty said, looking through his papers. "But, I don't really know what it means. It's in a long rant about nations being judged and that sort of thing."

"What do you make of it, Tiff?" asked Sammy.

"Well, I was just wondering if that's what's happening to Ty," she suggested.

Ty's eyebrows climbed up his forehead doubtfully. "What?" he asked sharply.

"Well, some people at my church think we are in the end times and all that," defended Tiff. "What if God is pouring out his Spirit on you and you're dreaming dreams?"

Tiff quickly averted her eyes to avoid Ty's glare while Lando began searching through his bag and bumped into Sammy as she sat, head bowed, concentrating on a drawing. The three friends quietly avoided Ty – not wanting to be on the receiving end of the outburst they knew was about hit.

"I can tell you logically why that is not true," Ty said.

Tiff released her breath as she listened to Ty's explanation.

"You see, as a Pastor's kid, I do know some things about the Bible and theology. If I were to believe in God, I would understand the quote to mean that in the end times, God would be pouring out his spirit on his believers. That would not include the likes of me." He smiled, and sat back in his chair, stretching his long legs way out under the table.

"But, Ty," insisted Tiff, "the quote says 'I will pour out my spirit on *all* people.' It doesn't specify believers. And I read the Quakers believe all people are born with what they called birth-right gifts from God."

"Well, it doesn't really matter," declared Ty. "Since God's existence cannot be proven,."

Tiff rolled her eyes; she was not going to back down. This made sense to her now and none of it made sense before. She needed them to understand, but she knew for Ty to hear, she had to tiptoe around the topic.

"Well, just to follow the thread, I looked up the word 'spirit,' and that led to the word 'gifts.' There are lots of different gifts the 'spirit' gives people. Maybe the spirit gave you dreams and Sammy visions."

"Visions?" asked Sammy.

"Your drawings," explained Tiff. "They're obviously not normal sketches. They contain information you could not possibly know."

Sammy sucked her bottom lip thoughtfully and exhaled. "I have to agree with Ty on this one. I doubt God would be giving *me* any gifts. Why would he give gifts to someone who hates him?"

"You hate God?"

"I have my reasons," Sammy's voice clipped sharply – cutting off further questions.

"Is anyone else hungry?" Lando cut in, easing the tension. "There's a coffee cart in here and snacks. I could use a break."

"Let's do it," agreed Ty eagerly, jumping to his feet and heading away from the table as fast as he could move. Lando was close behind.

"Well, it's an improvement," said Tiff as they scooted back their chairs to stand. "Ty is getting better at keeping his temper."

"Yeah," agreed Sammy. "Ty made it through the whole conversation without stomping off. That's impressive."

"Sammy, the boys really like this new look of yours. Do you think you might try it outside of work?" Tiff tried to push down the stab of jealousy that was threatening to bubble up when she thought of the appreciative way Ty gazed at her friend.

"I don't know. I'm pretty shocked by their reaction and yours too. Did I look *that* bad?"

Tiff took a good look at Sammy. The fear she saw in her friend brought a quick end her to her feelings of jealousy. "Today you look happy, care free – like somebody who could be a trusted friend. The gothic look makes you look secretive and unfriendly. Like you are hiding your true self."

Sammy tilted her head as she contemplated these words. "Carefree," she repeated. "Hm, that does describe how I've been feeling lately. But what do you mean about hiding my true self?"

Tiff chose her words carefully. Sammy was like a fawn coming out of the woods for food. Not wanting to frighten the skittish fawn away, Tiff softly murmured, "Well, the long sleeves, long pants, long hair in your face, are like a wall of protection warning people to 'stay away.'"

Sammy silently pursed her lips.

Tiff was afraid she'd blown it. She needed to salvage the moment if not repair the damage. "I like your lighter colors, but why are you still wearing long sleeves in this heat?"

Sammy stood quite still then, as if she were about to dive off a high board. Taking her right hand she pulled the lacy sleeve to the elbow on the left arm. The inside of her arm was covered with many thin white horizontal scars. She looked at Tiff and waited for her reaction. Tiff's eyes welled with tears and she threw her arms around Sammy, hugging her close. Sammy's body was stiff at first – as if she wasn't used to being touched. After her initial shock, she relaxed and hugged Tiff back.

"Sammy," Tiff barely breathed, pulling away from her friend but timidly reaching out to touch the lines on her arm, "these are battle-born badges. Whatever they represent, they're a part of who you are. Someday, when you're ready, you can tell me the story, but they don't make you ugly. They show you're a survivor. If I were you, I'd show them off as a sign that I lived to tell the tale." Without giving Sammy a clue to her intentions, Tiff quickly leaned in to place a light kiss on one of the scars.

Sammy inhaled sharply, pulled her arm back as if she'd been burned. Eyes welling with tears, she protectively held her arm to her chest.

Instantly, Tiff regretted the impulse. What if Sammy withdrew from her again? Afraid she'd made a terrible mistake, her mind screamed, *why did I do that? I've scared her.* She pleaded, "I'm sorry Sammy, I didn't mean to…"

"Thank you," came the soft reply.

"What?" asked Tiff in confusion.

"Tiff," Sammy said weakly, trying not to cry. "I don't have any more words right now, but thank you." She pulled down her sleeve and picked up her bookbag. "I think I'd like some of that coffee." Turning, she walked down the hall to the coffee cart.

Whew, thought Tiff, following. *That was a close one.*

CHAPTER EIGHTEEN
THE ORAL REPORT

MONDAY CAME TOO QUICKLY FOR THE BLUES, but Ty could tell they felt more confident than other groups even though they were going first. The parking lot was crammed with students who clustered in nervous circles trying to pin down last-minute project changes. When Mr. Monahan opened the door to the portable class-room, Ty turned to his friends for an impromptu pep talk. "Okay, listen up!" he began.

"Okay, Coach Dupree," chided Tiff, throwing her arms over Sammy and Lando and hunching them down like a football huddle.

"Funny," said Ty, "I was just going to say not to worry." Looking directly at Sammy, knowing public speaking was especially fearful for her, "We've all done our homework on this and we've gone over and over it. We know what we're talking about. It's a piece of cake. We are the Blue Group and we will stand tall together!"

"Right!" said Tiff, clapping her hands together loudly. "Hands in the middle! Hands in the middle!" She cheered, putting her right hand into the middle of the circle. The others reluctantly followed suit. "Okay on three, we say, 'Go Team Blue' – one, two, three!"

"Go Team Blue!" Tiff and Lando were loud with enthusiasm but Sammy and Ty had less. Ty shook his head as they ended their weak cheer. *Well, it's now or never.*

Turning toward the classroom, Tiff leaned into Sammy. "You look pretty today." Sammy was wearing the same Saturday outfit.

"Thanks," she whispered. "I feel pretty naked and I threw up this morning when I realized we're giving the report today. So I figured I may as well give in and go for it. Changing my look might distract from my horrible report!"

"You'll be fine. You look great and your part of the report is strong."

"Thanks, you look nice, too." Tiff did look uncharacteristically feminine today with a sporty, short white skirt and red tank top. Her hair was down, but pulled off her face by a fancy white headband. Linking arms, they marched up the steps to class.

Mr. Monahan waited for his students to settle down. "It's good to see you this beautiful day," he began. "Hey, Chandra, look at you wearing short sleeves! Is your blood finally thickening up?"

"I guess it is," her husky voice replied. "I actually feel warm today."

Mr. Monahan looked around at each member of the class, quickly checking that all were present as he did each morning. "Today begins our oral reports. I'm really looking forward to learning something from each of you." He glanced back at the board where the list of sign-ups was still visible. "First up we'll hear from the Blue Group." He watched as they gathered their papers and began to slowly walk to the front of the class. "Well, where is Sam today and who is this substituting for her?"

The class laughed and Sammy's pale cheeks blossomed with color. Mr. Monahan quickly added, "You look nice today, Sam. I'd like you all to notice that each member of the Blues has chosen to dress up a little for their report. I think that is awesome. If you were to give a report for a job or even a toast at a wedding, you would pay careful attention to your appearance. Excellent modeling! It's all yours."

Ty had been designated to go first. He stood tall in his khaki pants and short-sleeved, crewneck blue t-shirt. As he began, his smooth voice calmed the class and his teammates. All the students gave him their full attention.

"Our group has been interested in the area of dreams," he began. "It's a subject that came up in our journals." This was only a half truth, of course, but worked well for the report. "We have decided to look at dreams from four perspectives. I took my information from the Old Testament, Tiff researched the New Testament, Sammy covered the psychological aspects, and Lando will finish with the pop culture angle including statistics from our opinion poll. We interviewed twenty people about dreams. I'm sure there are other sources that we missed, but these are the ones we chose to study. So, I'll begin."

When it was Tiff's turn, she bounced into position with her usual enthusiasm. Sharing all she found in the New Testament regarding dreams, she lifted her eyes to make eye contact with her classmates, saying, "Each one on our team has a different opinion about the scripture I read to you from Acts. I was wondering what it would be like if God decided to give his gifts to all people, like it says here. Some people –" she glanced significantly at Ty who now stood to her right at the end of the Blue Group –"thought this passage was referring only to people who believed in God. I, however, am interested in the idea that it could happen to anyone. The passage says it could, regardless of their beliefs. My question is this, 'If it happened. If God suddenly gave you a special talent, would you recognize it?'" Her eyes traveled the room, making contact, drawing her classmates in.

Some reacted with "ohhh" and others looked off thoughtfully.

Then Tiff headed to the end of the line.

That was great, thought Tyrell, *leave them wanting more!*

When she stepped next to Ty, she gently swayed over to bump him, asking a non-verbal, "How'd I do?" He bumped her back with a reassuring but non-verbal, "Good job." They glanced at each other, his smile reflected in her own.

Sammy was next and took a deep breath, looking to her team for support before beginning. "My part of the report," she started only to be interrupted by Toby from the back of the room.

"Can't hear you," he said loudly. Some people giggled. Ty shot them a dirty look.

Sammy straightened her back, took another a deep breath and glanced at Lando who gave her a nod of support. Knocking her volume up a notch, she began again, but with more confidence and determination, "My part of the report has to do with the psychological perspectives on dreams."

Look at her, thought Ty. *She's like a butterfly emerging from her cocoon.* He watched her give her report with more confidence than he had ever imagined. When she was done, Sammy flashed a brilliant smile to her team and took her place beside Tiff at the end of the line. Tiff gently bumped her arm. Sammy bumped Tiff back and exhaled deeply. Ty felt his heart brimming with pride at how well his team was doing.

Lando took his place at the front. He wore a white button-down, short-sleeved shirt with his long, brown tailored shorts. Sammy smiled encouragingly at him. Ty noticed an extra sparkle in Lando's eye as he smiled back at Sammy and wondered, *is there something brewing between those two?*

Lando's sense of humor was strong in his presentation. He talked about books, movies, and TV shows that used dreams as part of a plot line. When he admitted to watching the movies based on Stephanie Meyer's vampire series, some of the guys in the class groaned.

"Hey, don't knock it 'til you've tried it!" he joked, and added, "Research, research!" Holding up a fist and chanted, "Team Jacob!"

This brought a lot of chatter from the class as they argued which Stephanie Meyer's character was best. Pro Edward and pro Jacob opinions bounced around the room. Ty had never read the series but heard enough from the girls at school to know what people were talking about. He was impressed with how Lando managed to control the crowd.

"Okay, okay" said Lando, easily reining them in. "Our opinion poll was probably more interesting to do than it was results-wise." He continued in a whiny voice, "I had to ask three random people on the bus in order to fill out my quota of five people. It was so embarrassing, I only asked cute girls!" again the class laughed with him.

He's a charmer, thought Ty. *He could be a politician and aren't politicians often lawyers? Maybe Tiff was right!*

Lando summarized the poll results, which were similar to the psychological findings mentioned before. He added the ethnic specific information they'd uncovered. Lowering his papers, he concluded, "That's all folks!"

Ty felt himself relax with relief because they had all done well!

Mr. Monahan approached them before they could make their escape. "Let's give the Blue Group a hand for their excellent work." He began clapping and the class joined in and cheered. "I think they have just set a high bar for the rest of you."

Sammy started toward her seat.

Mr. Monahan said, "Wait, wait. Now we gets to ask you questions." Looking at the class, he asked, "Is there anything you'd like to ask the Blue Group about their process or content?"

The room was silent. "Okay, I'll go first," he said. "I'd like to know how you came up with the initial idea to do a report on dreams."

The three turned in unison to Ty. He had to answer but not give too much away. How would he explain this? "Well," he said carefully, "I had a dream and wrote about it in my journal. When I shared it with our group, it led to a – well, let's say, a series of discussions about dreams. And that is why we decided we had to research the topic."

"Any other questions or comments for the Blues?" asked Mr. Monahan.

Amy, the beautiful African-American girl, spoke up, "I liked how you included the different ethnic opinions about dreams."

The group smiled and nodded in thanks.

A Latino boy named Ray raised his hand and said, "I'm interested in the question that Tiffany asked about the gifts coming on you. I'd like to know how each Blue Group member answered that question."

"I'm interested in that question as well," added Mr. Monahan.

Ty started to squirm and saw fearful looks on the faces of his friends, too. How much could they say without giving away too much of what they'd been experiencing? But Mr. Monahan saved the day.

"Actually, I'd like to hear what you all have to say to Tiffany's question. If God did something like that today, would you notice?"

Bullet dodged, thought Ty.

Amy raised her hand again, "I'd be on the side of God-followers being the ones who were getting the gifts," she said. "Why would he give gifts to people that don't follow him?"

"Good question," said Mr. Monahan. "What do *you* think?" lobbing the question back to the class.

Joshua piped up, "I think it would be like getting a super power. I'd want the gift of invisibility." The class laughed.

Mr. Monahan jumped in, "Joshua, do you think you'd notice if God gave you a special ability?"

"Of course."

"Why?" asked Mr. Monahan.

"Well, because it would be like you're going along in your normal old boring life and suddenly something would change. Like you're suddenly able to do or think something you couldn't do or think before. How could you not notice that, Dude?"

"Good observation, Dude," said Mr. Monahan. "Does anyone else have an opinion?"

Chandra spoke, "I think if God gave you a gift, whether or not you were a follower or a believer, the gift would have to be for something good. I mean, it would have to be something God would want you to do. Otherwise, what would be the point?"

"You mean like God would want you to smite someone?" said Toby loudly to a few laughs.

"No," said Chandra seriously. "I mean like help the homeless or overcome injustice or something, something Jesus-like."

"Interesting perspective," said Mr. Monahan. "I hope you keep discussing this amongst yourselves. Right now it's group time and the other three groups have a lot to live up to. So I'm sure you will want all your time. Tomorrow is," he glanced over his shoulder at the board, "the Red Group. As for you Blues, good job and you are dismissed early today." Everyone reacted with shock to this good news. "Yep, go home early or go celebrate your victory at Starbucks!"

The Blues headed back to collect their things, a huge smile on each member's face.

CHAPTER NINETEEN
THE RIDE

THE BLUE GROUP TROTTED FAST to the center of the parking lot before allowing their joy to explode with shrieks, jumps, high-fives and hugs. Not only had their report gone as well as they could hope, but they were free from class an hour and a half early.

"Dudes," Tiff squealed triumphantly, "that was awesome!"

"I'm so glad it's over," yelled Sammy.

"We rocked it," said Ty.

"We're awesome," said Lando, jumping up and down.

They stopped half-way across the parking lot and faced each other, still grinning. "What do you guys want to do? Lunch?" asked Ty.

Lando knew what they had to do. He'd felt it in his gut as soon as Mr. Monahan gave them the rest of the day off. But how was he going to convince the others? "Ty, do you have your car?"

"Yes, I do," Ty pointed at the nearby white Subaru. "Don't worry, Lando. I can give us a ride to lunch."

"Good," answered Lando seriously. "'Cept we're not going to lunch. We need to go up highway 80 to the first truck stop we see." The girls looked with shock at each other, then at Lando.

"Why?" asked Ty.

"I don't know how I know," began Lando, but to his surprise he was joined by a chorus of, "I just know!" as he finished his sentence. Staring at each other in silence, Ty rocked back on his feet.

"Listen you guys, I think all this spiritual stuff is OK but to go chasing up a mountain on a hunch? I don't know. It seems stupid. We have no proof of anything."

Lando was afraid Ty would resist, and, truthfully, he didn't have any proof of anything, just a feeling and heat radiating though his body. Deciding to try honesty, he acknowledged, "You're right Ty. I don't have any proof, just this strong feeling. But we've been sitting here talking about a girl who could be in trouble for over a week now and we have no idea what to do or how to help. Now we have an opportunity to do something, and I think we need to do it." Finishing, he looked at Sammy and Tiff for support.

"I agree," Tiff chimed in. "I'm sick of feeling helpless."

"Me too," agreed Sammy. "If there is something we can do, let's do it."

Ty glanced at his friends' faces, he was out-numbered. With a shrug and a nod indicating they follow, he headed for the car. Lando got in on the passenger side. The girls tumbled into the back.

Ty turned to face them. "The thing is: we have to get back by the end of class. We barely have time to get up to the first truck stop outside of Truckee. It will be cutting it close. I could give you all a ride home after if it helps."

"I'll take a ride," said Lando.

"I *have* to be back by the end of class," said Tiff. "My mom will be here to pick me up and if I'm not here, she'll freak."

"You could use my phone to call her," offered Ty.

"I have a phone. But, she'd kill me if she knew I left the school grounds at all. We need to be back on time."

"I have to be home on time too," agreed Sammy. "After class I pick up Charity."

"So," said Ty, looking intently at Lando. "Are you sure it's worth a drive up and down the mountain with very little time at the rest stop?"

Lando sat still, feeling the strong sensation in his body. "I'm sure."

"But how do you? Never mind," Ty said, turning the key to start the car. "It's a good thing I got gas yesterday." Ty pulled out of the high school parking lot and headed for I-80.

Lando said, "To be honest, I didn't think you'd go for it, Ty."

Ty didn't respond immediately. "I had another one of those damn dreams last night," he reluctantly admitted.

Tiff and Sammy leaned forward in their seats. "Did you get any new information?" asked Tiff.

"Well, you know how the dream starts? I'm walking up the mountain through the pine trees and then I'm at a rest stop."

"Yeah," Tiffany encouraged.

"Well, last night I saw a sign for Truckee before I saw the rest stop sign."

"Holy Canolie!" said Tiff.

"Holy Canolie?" asked Lando. "What happened to Shikie?"

"I'm over it," said Tiff matter-of-factly. "Do you guys think we'll find her there today? Dawna, I mean?"

The car got quiet. "What do you imagine doing if we *do* find her?" asked Ty. "Tell her to get in the car, quick? Then what? Will one of us take her home? Do we take her to the police? What if she won't come with us?"

"I'll take her home," Sammy stated calmly.

Everyone was quiet. Lando imagined showing up at his house with a strange girl who might be a prostitute – that wouldn't go over very well in his family.

"So *that's* our plan?" asked Ty indignantly, turning up the westbound freeway on-ramp. "We go up there, see Dawna and tell her to get in so she can go home with Sammy, who she doesn't even know!"

"I think we should go see what we see," suggested Lando. "There's no guarantee we'll see Dawna at all."

"But you said we had to go today," accused Ty, his temper ramping up.

"I did, but I did not say what we'd find when we got there," said Lando defensively.

"I think we should just enjoy the ride," cut in Tiff. "How often do we get a chance to hang together outside of school? All we know is that we're supposed to go to the rest area, so let's do that and chill till we get there."

"Yeah," said Lando, thankful for Tiff's idea. He didn't want Ty to get mad and turn around. "Let's talk about the oral report."

Ty seemed slightly put out by this sudden change of direction in the conversation, but he let it go.

"You were great, Lando," said Sammy admiringly.

Lando replied, "What about you? You didn't get sick or pass out or anything! You were great."

Sammy's face turned red, "I did actually get sick this morning, but seeing you all there with me helped a lot."

"I didn't know you were so funny, Lando," said Tiff.

Lando smiled widely, "I was, wasn't I?"

They all laughed, even Ty. He joined in, "Hey Tiff, the class really liked your question. It caused a lot of discussion."

"Yeah, what do you guys think about what Travis said?" asked Tiff.

"You mean about having super powers?" asked Lando. "I'm in."

"No," corrected Tiff. "Remember what he said about how if it happened to you – if God did put his spirit on you – you'd know it because you'd be going through your normal life and BAM! Something completely different would happen."

"I don't think he said BAM," Ty smiled.

"You know what I mean," chided Tiff. "What do you think about it?"

"Well," ventured Sammy, "it does sorta seem like what's happened to us. I mean, we were going along through our normal lives and suddenly things changed for each one of us."

"I like what Chandra said," added Tiff, "about how if God were to give you a bit of himself, you know, share some of his power, then you'd do stuff he would do. You sort of become his agent, acting for him, as he would."

"Yeah," smiled Ty, "like, smite people."

Tiff leaned forward and smacked Ty on the shoulder. "No, like helping people in trouble."

"Hey, no hitting the driver." Ty's hands flew up, off the wheel, in protest.

Lando yelled, "Hey, just drive, Driver!"

The sun and beauty of the mountains surrounded them. They were rehashing the report, which kept them talking happily for the first part of the trip, but as they approached the town of Truckee, they got quiet. The knot in Lando's stomach was now from nerves, not from his "knowing" sensation.

"It's about another ten miles up, I think," said Ty.

Lando wondered what would happen if they actually did find a girl who needed their help. The next thing he knew, Ty was taking an off-ramp labeled "Rest Stop."

"I'm so nervous," squeaked Tiff in a high-pitched voice. "I really gotta pee!"

"Me too," agreed Sammy, shivering despite the warmth of the car.

Pulling into the rest area, they nervously surveyed the scene. It was quickly apparent they had the area to themselves – no other cars were parked in the lot. "I don't know if I should be disappointed or relieved," Tyrell said.

"I don't either, but we need to pee. Come on, Sammy." Tiffany and Sammy flung open the doors and ran towards the women's bathrooms. The building had a narrow entrance with an uncovered hallway and doors on each side, women on the right and men on the left.

"Do you think we should at least look around, Ty?" asked Lando. "See what's in the back maybe?"

"I guess," said Ty, opening his door. The boys decided to circle the buildings so they wouldn't miss something important.

"WELL, NOBODY IS IN HERE," said Tiff, looking under the stalls for feet as she and Sammy washed their hands.

"I wonder why we came," asked Sammy. "Really, this is just one of many, many rest stops up here. This one doesn't even have truck parking spaces."

"Do you think it's the wrong one?" asked Tiff as they headed for the door.

Stepping out into the bright sunlight after their eyes had adjusted to the dark bathroom was almost painful. Standing outside the restroom blinking their eyes, they were physically startled when they heard a deep voice close to them.

"Hello ladies."

The girls instinctively stepped closer to each other, looking at the man leaning against the wall near the men's restroom. About twenty years old they guessed, he was handsome, about medium height, with blonde hair and bright blue eyes. Wearing jeans and a polo shirt, he looked casual, but in a practiced way. The girls froze in place, unsure of what to do.

The man took a step towards them. "I couldn't help but notice what beauty God has dropped into the High Sierras this lovely day, so I thought I'd stop and introduce myself."

Tiff shivered, and not from the crisp mountain air. This was not just a random encounter and she knew it. "Hi," she said tentatively, grabbing Sammy's arm to leave.

He stepped toward them, blocking their way to the car.

Where are the boys? wondered Tiff.

"My name's Chad Michaels," he offered along with his hand. The girls just looked at him until he finally put his hand down. "Nothing to fear girls," he cooed, putting his hands up in an 'I surrender' gesture. "I'm from Los Angeles and I work as a talent scout for a modeling agency called Comet Rising. Have you ever heard of us?"

"No," Tiff challenged, "but we have to go now."

"Already?" he asked, moving a half-step closer. "At least let me give you my card," he replied, calmly reaching into the back of his jeans.

Tiff tensed, afraid of what was coming next, but he pulled out a business card, stretching his hand toward her.

Carefully, she took the card, glancing at it quickly. It looked legitimate. Chad focused his gaze on Tiff. "Our agency represents a lot of Asian models. They're a hot commodity right now. When his eyes raked over her body, she almost lost her breakfast. He turned his gaze to Sammy and Tiff sensed Sammy's body stiffen.

"We could use you in our Indy section. Your look is current." He smiled, but the smile didn't reach his cold, blue eyes.

Hearing footsteps and Lando's booming laugh, both girls sighed heavily in relief.

"Well," Chad said with false cheer, "I really would like to work with you. Call me!" he offered as a farewell, placing his fingers to his ear as if it were a phone and turning around toward the parking lot.

"There you are," said Ty as he and Lando approached the girls from the opposite direction. "We thought you'd fallen in," he teased until he got closer and saw terror on their faces. "You two alright?"

"A guy," was all that Tiff could say as she pointed to the parking lot. Hearing a car engine rev up, Lando ran full speed in the direction she had pointed.

He shouted, "Stop, come back!"

Ty moved close to the girls to protect them until Lando's return.

"He's gone," Lando panted. "He was in a white van!"

"What?" said Ty in disbelief. "Did you get the license plate?"

"It was covered in mud."

Ty rattled off questions to the girls. "Did he hurt you? Are you okay? Did he have a red beard? Where did he come from?"

Tiff laughed nervously, despite herself. "We're okay!" she assured him. "And no, he didn't hurt us. And no, he didn't have a red beard. And I have no idea where he came from. He was suddenly just there in front of us."

"What did he say?" demanded Ty.

"He wanted us to join his modeling agency," she said, holding the card Chad had given her for Ty to take.

Studying the card, he asked, "Was he legitimate?"

"No," Tiff answered sharply before looking at Sammy who was nodding in agreement, and she quickly added, "Definitely sketch."

"Sketch?" asked Lando.

"Janky," explained Tiff. Lando still looked confused.

"Fake," Ty offered his interpretation. "I bet this is how they lure girls. Maybe we can catch him."

They ran to the car and climbed in, Tiff yelled "shotgun" and climbed into the front seat. Ty backed out the car and tore up the pavement toward the freeway entrance. Traffic was light, mostly eighteen-wheelers on their way over the mountain. There was no white van in sight as they drove west.

"Now," Ty asked Tiff, "tell me *exactly* what happened."

LANDO GLANCED AT SAMMY WHO, he realized, had not said one word since they'd gotten in the car. Shivering, her arms were clutched tightly around her chest while she rocked gently back and forth. Unzipping his backpack, he pulled out a fuzzy zip-up sweatshirt. "Here," he offered. "You look cold."

Lando watched her zombie-like movements as she obediently pulled on the sweatshirt. "You should fasten your seat belt," he softly suggested, watching her as she did so. "Sammy, are you okay?" he whispered. Unfastening his seat belt, scooting into the middle seat to be closer to her, he quickly rebuckled himself. She looked at him. Her eyes slowly refocused on his face as if coming back from a faraway place.

"I froze," she said in a barely audible voice.

"What?" he asked, leaning closer to hear her better.

"I froze," she repeated.

Lando glanced quickly toward Ty and Tiff but they were intently scanning the road for white vans. Lando turned back to Sammy. "You're safe now, Sammy. You're gonna be okay." He gently put his warm arm around her.

Turning her shoulders toward him, her eyes pleading, she spoke in hushed tones, "But, don't you see, Lando, I said I'd never let it happen again. I planned so many scenes in my mind. I'd run, I'd scream, I'd fight. Anything to get away; instead, I just froze." A tear slid down her cheek as she looked at him with eyes overflowing with pain.

Lando sat quietly for a moment trying to think of what he could possibly say to help her. Pulling his arm from her shoulder to turn her face close to his, he asked, "Sammy, can I tell you a secret?"

The intimate question brought Sammy back from her hiding place and she saw Lando, really saw him for the first time. "Of course," she whispered back.

"I'm a bastard," he confided quietly.

"What? What do you mean? You're one of the nicest guys I know."

He shook his head, realizing that she had misunderstood. "Remember I told you that my uncle, brothers and my grandpa were killed by the soldiers in El Salvador?

"Yes," she said.

"Well, it wasn't really my Uncle Tomas. He was my mom's husband, the father of my two brothers who were killed."

"I'm so sorry Lando. You lost your father, too?"

"Well, not exactly. I told you my mom and grandma were both raped by the soldiers, right?"

"Yes."

"That is how I came to be," he finished, looking at his lap, filled with the shame of what he'd never shared with anyone before. Scared to see what he feared would be in Sammy's eyes, he couldn't find the courage look at her. Not knowing if his confession would help her, he hadn't known what else to say, but it was all he had to give. A gentle hand caressed his arm. Startled, he looked up to find Sammy's watery eyes. She gazed at him with a soft smile and squeezed his arm.

"Thanks Lando," she whispered. "And Lando, I'm sorry for what your mother had to endure, but I'm glad you came to be, no matter how it happened." With that, she released his arm and turned toward the window.

"Guys," said Ty from the front seat. "I'm afraid I have bad news. We haven't seen the guy or the van and we are running out of time to get you all home before class ends. We've got to turn back."

Lando and Sammy both nodded. It was time to go back.

CHAPTER TWENTY
SAM'S STORY

TUESDAY STARTED WITH ITS SHARE of disappointment for Sammy. Secretly, she had hoped Mr. Monahan would continue to give them time off since they'd finished their report. Unfortunately, he only allowed the group that was giving their report that day to take time off. All of the others were either supposed to work on their reports or share from their journals.

After class they sprawled out on the grass in the warm June sunlight. Sammy was wearing a short-sleeve shirt for the first time that summer. Because her arms were so pale and thin, her scars were not the first thing a person noticed, but Lando did notice them. In his usual way, he directly asked about them. "Sammy, how did you get those scars?"

Sammy looked carefully into his brown eyes, noting no judgment in them. She decided it was time to tell her story. These people had stuck by her, laughed and fought with her. They were the closest thing to real friends she'd ever had. She took a shaky breath and began.

"I cut myself, Lando," she glanced at Tiff, who nodded in support. Ty sat up to listen as Lando leaned closer. She continued. "When I was ten, my mom married a bad man. At night he started coming to my room and made me do terrible things. My mom was drinking then, so he waited until she passed out before he'd come in. He said if I told her, or anyone else, he'd hurt Charity." A tear slid down Sam's face. When she sneaked a glance into Lando's eyes, she was surprised to see his eyes were glistening with moisture too. Tiff had tears rolling down her face faster than she could brush them away and Ty looked ready to kill someone or something. Encouraged, Sammy felt understood by her friends' responses.

"Finally, when I was twelve and Charity was two, he made a comment that she would soon be old enough to join in our 'little games.' That's what he called them, 'our little games.'"

"Oh," said Tiff, holding her stomach like she'd been gut-punched. Ty moved closer to Tiff, putting his hand on her back. Tiff nodded to him that she was okay and reached out to touch Sammy's hand. Sammy squeezed Tiff's hand in acknowledgement and continued with her story.

"That," she said with fiery eyes, "was never, never going to happen." Lando nodded with understanding. "I waited until school the next day and then marched right into my school counselor's office and told her everything. It was the hardest thing I've ever done. The police came and eventually he went to jail."

"You are so brave," said Lando with both admiration and awe in his voice.

"I'm so proud of you, Sammy," agreed Tiff. "You have guts!"

Sammy soaked in each word. "Well, I might not have done it if I'd known what would happen next. Foster homes with strangers became our life; at least we were allowed to stay together, but the hardest was when I had to testify in court. I had to see a therapist and relive the abuse and embarrassment over and over." Sammy slipped away into her memories until the silence around her roused her to shake her head and sit up straight. "But, I guess it was worth it. He's in jail and we have Dirk now. He's better. And Mom is clean and Charity is having a better childhood than I did. So that's good," she proclaimed, but her voice went up at the end as if she wasn't quite sure.

"And the scars?" asked Lando, lifting her tiny wrist and turning it over in his hands.

"I started cutting myself when I was about twelve. I think it helped me somehow be sure I was alive and could feel things. I'd gotten so zombied out"

Lando nodded in understanding. "My grandmother has scars too. After the soldiers raped her and she saw that they were going to rape my mother, she fought them with all her might. They knocked out some of her teeth and hit her with the barrels of their guns." He drew slash marks across his face and arms to indicate how his grandmother had been hit. "She says her scars are reminders that a person can hurt your body, but no one can take your spirit away from you."

Sam looked down at the scars on her arms. "I guess that's true, but I feel like my spirit almost didn't make it." She was quiet, remembering the pain of those days.

"But you did! Look at you." Ty spoke fast, "You're alive and free and you protected your sister! You are brave. You didn't give up and that slime bucket is in jail. You put him there. You're amazing!" He beamed at her.

"Yes, you are," Tiff agreed. She grabbed hold of Sammy's arm and took a felt pen from her backpack. Holding out Sammy's arm, she wrote the word LOVED in big letters all across the scars. "And, you are loved!"

"Yes, you are," agreed Lando, "loved."

Sammy's throat felt tight. She bit her lip and tried not to cry even more. Looking down at her arm, she traced the letters. It felt as if the door of her internal cage was being pried open by her friends.

Sammy returned Tiff and Lando's smiles, but when she looked at Ty, he was staring at Tiff in a most amazed and loving way. Sammy averted her eyes, embarrassed to have glimpsed Ty's private emotions. Then she realized that Tiff and Lando were still waiting for her to speak. "Thanks," she said, feeling shy again. "I do feel a lot better these days since I met you guys." She sat quietly again. Always uncomfortable when the attention focused on her for too long, she changed the subject. "Now we have to help another girl who is in even worse trouble. Anybody have any ideas?"

Ty said, "I looked up this phony modeling agency online. It doesn't exist. It's frustrating because it's like we have enough information to go to the police, but since the whole thing is based on dreams and drawings, they won't take us seriously.. If Sammy or I could just dream or draw a license plate, we'd have a better case."

"I'll get right on it," smiled Sammy.

Ty turned to Lando, "Have any more strong feelings about what we should do next?"

"Unfortunately, no. Do you think we should just drive around from rest stop to rest stop and look for her?"

"Maybe," said Ty, "but it seems to go better when you have one of your 'knowings.'"

"I hate this," said Sammy. "Dawna is out there somewhere, in trouble, and we have to sit here waiting for some sort of 'divine' information before we can help her."

"Well, in the meantime, does anyone want to share from their journal?" asked Tiff.

CHAPTER TWENTY-ONE
ROAD TRIP

THE ROAD WAS DARK AND FAMILIAR. Ty passed the sign that said Rest Stop and took the exit. This was the rest stop his family usually took when coming over the mountain on the way home from visiting his aunt in Sacramento. His sisters' bladders could never make it all the way over the mountain. This rest stop was big and well-lit and often had parked cars no matter how late you stopped. Something felt different to him this time. Urgent. Shuddering, he realized he should not have come up here alone. Why didn't he at least bring Lando with him? This was dangerous; he was sure of it. Yet, he'd felt compelled to leave his bed in the middle of the night and drive up the mountain in search of Dawna. Pulling into the well-lit rest stop, he saw trucks lining the left side in neat parking spaces. A car was parked to his right. *Is someone in the restroom?*

He stopped his car near the other one. *Safety in numbers,* he thought. Unfortunately for him, two girls came out of the women's side of the rest stop bathroom and headed for the car. They eyed him nervously as they opened their car doors and pulled quickly out of the rest stop. *No safety for the black guy,* he thought sadly. *Well, I'm here. I might as well look around.*

He opened the car door and stepped out into the night. Looking down the row of trucks he saw their dim parking lights on and heard the low rumble of their engines. *Great. If a trucker finds me poking around his truck at two a.m., I'm dead!* He tried to walk soundlessly down the row of trucks, straining his eyes for anything that might give him a clue. One truck drew his gaze. It was a huge, dark-blue truck with the word *Wagner* on the side. The front of the cab looked like the face of a bulldog. As he got closer, he heard shouting. Stepping nearer, he strained his ears to try to hear. He could hear the deep rumble of a man's voice and the high-pitched voice of a girl, but the engine drowned out the words. He thought his heart would burst out of his chest it was vibrating so hard, the tremors beginning to shake his whole body. Was he having a heart attack? Looking down at his chest, he saw only blackness, and real panic surged, making it hard to breathe. Suddenly, he was jerked upward as his heart burst from his chest, flying through the air as his hand reached to catch it. Fingers closed around his throbbing heart, only to feel its beating still. Blackness closed in, but there was no pain, just remorse that he had failed Dawna.

Slowly, Ty became aware, but where was he? Was there really life after death? Suddenly, his heart began to vibrate and he reached to put it back in his chest. His eyes popped open when he recognized the feel of his cell phone vibrating louder now that he had lifted his body off of it. A dim green light created eerie familiar shadows. With eyes wide and pupils dilated to let in every scrap of light, he recognized his own bedroom. His phone had been under his chest where he'd rolled on top of it in his sleep. Smashing his face into his pillow while trying to look down during the dream, he had pressed his face into the pillow and almost smothered himself. It had been so real and then gotten so bizarre! Squinting at the clock, he fumbled for his phone as it began to vibrate again. It was one A.M. He hit the answer button and whispered, "Yeah?"

"Ty, it's Lando."

"What's up?" Ty was afraid he already knew the answer to his question.

"We have to go now," Lando answered urgently.

There was no doubt in Ty's mind this time. He made no argument. "Okay, I'll come get you."

The phone was silent as Lando sat, seemingly stunned at Ty's quick acquiescence. "What about the girls?" Lando asked once he'd recovered.

"I think we should leave them. This is dangerous."

"No, we have to take them."

Ty did not want to do this. He was afraid enough for himself, but he sure didn't want to drag the girls into a dangerous situation. "Lando, are you sure that you're sure? I really don't feel good about taking them."

"I'm sure that I'm sure."

"But –"

"Ty, we don't have time to argue. We need to go now. I don't know how I know. You have to trust me on this."

Ty was still. If he hadn't had that dream, he wouldn't have been persuaded, but now he knew Lando was right. He had to trust him. "Okay, you call them and I'll come get you first. I'm on my way." He hung up the phone before Lando could reply.

"If my parents find out, I'm toast," said Tiff as she slid into Ty's backseat behind Lando.

"Are you afraid to come?" asked Ty.

"Not really. It was weird: as soon as Lando called, I knew we'd go tonight. It felt right, like now was the time."

"Well, it seems we're all sure of that," said Ty.

"I was sure I'd get caught when I snuck out, but no one made a sound. How did you get talked into this, Ty?"

He repeated his dream for the second time that night.

Tiff quivered, "That gives me the shivers!"

They drove in silence in the stillness of night until they headed past the high school and up to Sammy's apartment complex. She was waiting for them, sitting, small and hunched, on the curb.

"What set off the alarm?" she asked as she slid into the back seat with Tiff.

Ty tried not to stare, but Sammy had surprised him once again. She had shown up without makeup, wearing baggy pajama pants and a sweatshirt, looking about twelve years old. No one commented on it.

Lando said, "I was sound asleep but woke up knowing we all had to go, now!"

Ty continued, "I had a dream and I know which rest area we need to go to. In my dream, I could hear a guy and a girl arguing in one of the trucks. Then Lando called."

"It feels right to me," Tiff added, shrugging her shoulders.

"Okay, this is it. We couldn't ask for more guidance than that."

"Unless you've drawn something new?" asked Ty.

"Sorry, no."

"So, what do we do when we get there?" asked Lando.

"I was hoping you'd know," Ty fired back.

"You're the one with the dreams," Lando griped .

"You're the one who woke me up in the middle of my dream before I could figure out what to do."

"Guys," said Tiff, "we can't attack each other because it's late and we're scared. We have to hang together. Let's just drive up there and see what happens."

"What choice do we have?" agreed Sammy.

"Sorry," said Ty, glancing at Lando.

"Sorry," echoed Lando.

They remained fairly quiet during their second trip up the mountain in one week. This time they had to drive further, all the way to Donner Summit. Then had to turn around and head back east to catch the rest stop Ty saw in his dream. After exiting the freeway to make the direction change, Ty felt his nerves jump to high alert and pulled to the side of the road, turning to face them.

"What are you doing?" asked Lando.

"I don't know. It's just that this could be dangerous. I think we should have some rules about what we're doing."

"Rules?" asked Sammy. "Like what?"

"Well, like we stick together this time. No separating."

"Good idea," agreed Lando.

"Anything else?" asked Tiff. The car was quiet as they sat thinking. Ty could tell he wasn't the only one dreading what came next. The air in the car was crackling.

When no one spoke he pulled the car back onto the highway and took the truck stop off-ramp. "Here it is." He reached down and turned off his headlights, letting the car quietly roll forward.

"Maybe we should call the police." whispered Tiff.

"Not yet," said Ty. "We need more information." He drove into the rest stop. The car side of the parking lot was mostly empty, but the truck side was almost full. Two girls came out of the women's restroom and got into the lone car to leave.

"Damn," said Ty, "those girls were in my dream."

"That's a good thing," Sammy said. "It means we're supposed to be here."

"I guess, but it's spooky."

Instead of parking, he decided to continue inching through the parking lot. As he got to where the trucks were parked, he rolled down his window. "We have to listen for the yelling."

Three other windows were rolled down simultaneously. They heard nothing but the sound of the diesel engines and distant traffic.

Ty stopped suddenly and pointed at a dirty, dark-blue truck about four trucks ahead. "That's the one, the blue one with the snubbed-nose front." He took a breath and let the car roll forward.

"I can hear voices!" said Lando as they got to the back of the blue truck. "I can hear the yelling. What should we do?" He had his hand on the door handle poised to jump out.

"Wait!" said Ty in a panicked voice. Lando let go of the handle. "Remember, we all stick together."

Lando nodded.

Ty stopped when they could see the passenger door of the truck. The voices were louder. They heard a high-pitched voice yell, "No, I won't!"

An angry male voice said, "I paid good money for this!"

"I can't. Please don't make me." the girl's voice begged. The eyes of those in the car got bigger as they heard the girl start to sob. Ty felt panic swelling in his chest. *What should we do? Jump out? Pound on the truck door?*

"Ah, just get out!" yelled the man's voice.

Before they knew what happened, the passenger door of the truck was flying open and a skinny blonde girl fell out onto the asphalt. Her purse was thrown out after her. She hit the pavement hard and didn't move. She lay crying with her head on the ground.

Is that it? wondered Ty. *We just pick her up and go?*

"What did you do now, you little bitch?" This voice came from their right. All four tore their eyes away from the girl on the ground and looked into the darkness on the right. A large man with a beard moved into a circle of light at the far end of the car parking area. Behind him, barely discernable in the dark, was a white van. The guy was about twenty-five yards away, moving fast toward them. "Angel, you get back in there right now or I'll kick your ass myself."

Sammy acted before anyone could stop her. She opened the car door and moved a half-step toward the girl sprawled on the ground weeping. "Angel," she whispered. The girl didn't move away from the ground. "Dawna," she said in a louder voice. This time the girl looked up through her hair at the sound of her name. Sammy pleaded, "Quick, get in the car. We're here to help you!"

Dawna looked at her, uncomprehending, and then staggered to her feet and looked to the white van and the man.

"Who's there?" shouted the large man, who had covered half the distance and could now see their car in the shadows of the trucks. He began to run toward them.

"Dawna, please," begged Sammy. "We've come to help you." She stretched out her hand toward Dawna. With one last look at the man shouting and running toward them, Dawna looked back at Sam's outstretched hand and hesitated.

"Sammy," shouted Ty. "Get back in the car, hurry!"

The man was fifteen feet away, but Sammy tried again, "Dawna, hurry!"

"I'll kill you, bitch! Don't you touch that girl. She's mine!"

Dawna made a decision. She moved toward Sammy and grabbed her hand. Sammy pulled Dawna toward her and pushed her into the back seat. Tiff pulled her further in and buckled her into the middle. Sammy tried to follow, but the man caught up to the car and launched himself across the back of the car's trunk toward her. He snagged her left arm, holding on and swearing as he balanced on the back of the car. Sammy's face was red with pain and rage. Before anyone could act, she sunk her teeth into his meaty arm and bit down as hard as she could. He let go of Sammy's arm and yelled.

"You bitch!" he screamed, but before he could move from on top of the car, Lando popped out of the door and around the back. He looked like a cage fighter as he grabbed the big man by the belt and yanked with all his might shouting, *"¡NO! ¡Ningunas mujeres van a estar lastimadas en mi reloj!"* – No! No women are going to be hurt on my watch!

He tossed the guy off the car onto the hard pavement. Simultaneously, Sammy jumped in the car and Lando dashed back to his side, with the slamming doors sounding like gun shots.

"Drive," screamed Lando, and Ty hit the gas pedal.

Behind them, the red-bearded man was staggering to his feet. "Come back here!" he yelled before turning to shout, "Johnny! Johnny!" He frantically gestured for the driver to come to him as he limped back toward the white van. Ty saw the headlights pop on and a light-colored cargo van pull out of the darkness to stop and pick up the raging, bearded guy.

"Faster, they're coming after us!" yelled Lando.

The van flung gravel as the driver stomped on the accelerator before red-beard got his door closed.

"What should we do?" asked Tiff.

"Please don't let him take me back, please!" Dawna begged from the back seat in a slurred voice.

"Dawna, are there more girls in that van?" asked Sammy.

"What?" asked Dawna. Her eyes were half closed and she seemed confused by the question.

"In the van," repeated Sammy. "Are there more kidnapped girls in the back of that van?"

"How do you know?" asked Dawna. "Who are you? How do you know my name?"

"They're gaining on us!" yelled Lando.

Ty looked at the lights getting closer in his rearview mirror. "There's no way my car can outrun them."

"Dawna, listen," asked Sammy urgently. "We'll explain that later, but right now I need to know if there are more girls in that van."

"Yes," said Dawna slowly, "two more."

"Then we have to call the police!" said Tiff with confidence. "We have to call them now!" Ty and Lando exchanged looks. Ty gave his head a quick nod.

Tiff dialed 9-1-1. "Yes, I need the highway patrol," she said in an amazingly calm voice.

The white van was on the bumper of the Subaru now. Its lights glared down into the car.

"Yes, I'm on highway 80 headed east just past Donner area, west of Truckee. And there is a white van driving like a madman is behind the wheel." said Tiff into the phone. "I think the driver might be drunk. He's tail-gating me as we speak. It's like he is trying to hit my car or push me off the road and I'm scared."

Ty was using all his concentration to keep his car on the road and ahead of the white van. Part of his mind was trying to process what Tiff was saying. Why didn't she say they were being chased by crazed kidnappers? Why was she being so calm?

The van hit the bumper of the Subaru and the car jolted forward. "Yikes! He just hit me!" said Tiff, letting her rising panic resonate into the phone. "He's getting really close. I don't know how I can stay in front of him!"

The van swerved into the fast lane and started to gain on the Subaru. Ty looked around. Should he slam on the brakes? Spin around and drive the wrong way on the freeway? No, that was suicide. He tried for more power but the car could not out-pace the van. Tiff's calm voice continued to register in some part of his brain. *What is she doing?*

"He's trying to pass me," said Tiff into the phone. "The guy driving is young, about twenty, and blonde. The guy in the passenger side is big with a red beard. No, I'm not driving."

The van pulled quickly into the lane ahead of the Subaru and Ty swerved onto the shoulder to avoid being hit. His tires slid on the gravel and he almost hit the retaining wall. Gripping the wheel hard, he slowed down and pulled back into the lane behind the white van. Suddenly it dawned on him what Tiff was doing. She was trying to keep them from having to talk directly to the police. She was trying to act as though she was just reporting a drunk driver, trying to keep Dawna out of it. *What a girl!*

"They're coming up behind us now?" asked Tiff in surprise. She turned to look back into the dark mountain air for a patrol car. Ty glanced in the rearview mirror and saw nothing but darkness. Tiff closed the phone with a click as she scanned the black mountain behind her.

Lando turned to look, too, but they were all jolted forward as Ty slammed on the brakes and swerved left to avoid the van that had hit its breaks and tried to ram them.

"Ty!" shouted Tiff. "Just stay away from him a few more minutes. She said the highway patrol is right behind us."

Ty moved into the fast lane, but now the white van was slowing down alongside of him again. "That could be easier said than done." He tried to speed up to pass the white van. Again it veered toward him trying to push him off the highway. Suddenly, bright lights and sirens were directly behind them, as not one, but two, highway patrol cars crested the hill.

"Whew," said Ty, slowing down. The van, however, did not slow down. In fact, it sped up, trying to outrun the police, and both patrol cars followed on its tail. Ty took the next exit and pulled to the side of the road. He stopped the car, panting. They sat, silently collecting their breaths.

"Shikey," said Lando.

"Please don't take me to the police," begged Dawna. "I just want to go home. Please!"

Ty had almost forgotten Dawna sitting in the back between the girls. He turned to look at her now. He couldn't see her well in the dark, but what he could see of her was a frightened mess. *Now what?* "Where is home?"

"Sierraville," she said.

"Where's Sierraville?" he asked.

"Not that far away – could you take me home? Please?"

Dawna having a home and family was not something Ty had even considered. His brain was too ramped up on adrenaline to even know how to answer her. He had to think. *What should I do?*

CHAPTER TWENTY-TWO
THE REVELATION

TIFF SAT IN THE BACK SEAT NEXT TO Dawna and Sammy. She tried to slow her breathing. Her hands were shaking hard. *Relax,* she told herself, *it's over.* Ty and Lando unbuckled their seat belts and faced the girls. Tiff heard a third highway patrol car go screaming past on the freeway above them. Ty turned on the dome light.

"I hope those girls are okay," said Sammy.

"Me, too," agreed Tiff. She could barely let herself think about the other two girls trapped in that speeding van. *God, protect them!*

"What do you guys think we should do?" asked Ty as he typed something into his cell phone.

"Do we need to talk to the police?" asked Lando.

"I don't know," said Ty.

"Please don't turn me in," begged Dawna. "I just want to go home. I'll never run away again. I promise."

This was the first time they'd all been able to see each other in the light. Dawna had mascara streaming down her face, which was puffy from crying, and her hair was a tangled mess. She had scrapes on her cheek, hands and knees where she'd fallen on the asphalt from the truck. Her eyes looked like she'd been drugged. Ty opened his glove box and pulled out a little first aid kit, handing it to Tiff.

"And home is Sierra-something?" asked Tiff, trying to keep Dawna's mind off the pain she was about to feel. She opened the box, taking out cotton swabs and a small bottle of peroxide. She kept dabbing at Dawna's wounds as she waited for an answer. Dawna winced away from Tiff and closed her eyes.

"Sierraville," said Ty, looking at his phone. It's about an hour and a half from here up highway 89. It will take about an hour to get to Reno from there. It's two-thirty now, which would get us home around five, if we're lucky. What do you guys think?"

"I'm for taking her home," said Sammy.

"What about the police?" asked Tiff.

"Tiff," questioned Tyrell, "You didn't tell them anything about us. You say what kind of car we were in or anything?"

"No, I didn't." Tiff tried to remember. "I was trying to sound, you know, like a concerned citizen reporting a drunk driver."

"Cool," said Lando. "So, we could maybe just keep on driving and not need to talk to them? I don't want my mom to know I was out here tonight."

Sammy sat up in the seat, "What if those girls need us? We have to help them, even if we all get in trouble."

"You're right," agreed Lando.

"Please," begged Dawna, "I just want to go home."

Tiff draped an arm around her. "Ty, where is the turn off to Sierraville?"

"About ten miles up the road."

Tiff looked at Dawna, as if weighing something important. She wanted to take Dawna home but knew that the safety of the other two girls was more important. "Well, why don't we just keep going and see what we see. Then, if we get to the turn-off but don't see the van, we'll call the cops to check on the girls." She swallowed loudly, "Even if it means we have to turn ourselves in. But, if we see them and the police have the girls, we keep driving. The turn-off will be our deciding point."

Ty looked at Lando and Sammy, "What do you two think?"

"Let's do it," said Lando.

"Sam?"

"I'm ready."

Ty started up the engine and headed out. Five miles down the road they saw flashing lights. Ty slowed his car, moving into the fast lane away from the lights. As they drove by, they could see the white van had been forced off the road by the patrol cars. The young man calling himself Chad at the rest stop was the van driver; Johnny was sitting in the back of one of the patrol cars. Two officers had the red-bearded man handcuffed and lying against the top of a patrol car. In front of the two patrol cars, an officer was taking statements from two young, disheveled girls.

"They're going to be okay, Dawna," said Tiff with relief in her voice. Dawna was slouched down in her seat. "Look, Dawna!"

Dawna peeked over the back seat at the girls with the officers. "Good," she began to sob.

It took a long time for Dawna to stop crying once she started. Both Sammy and Tiff had wet shoulders before she was cried out. When she stopped, she said, "I'm sorry, guys, but I really gotta pee!"

Sammy and Tiff laughed in relief, sharing a look of agreement around Dawna.

Lando rolled his eyes, "What is it with girls and pee?"

"Hey, we have smaller bladders," said Tiff.

Ty pulled off the freeway at the next gas station and the girls went into the bathroom together. When Dawna emerged, she looked much better. She wore Lando's zip-up sweatshirt over her short jean shorts and red halter top. Ty bought snacks for everyone. Back in the car, Dawna ate like she hadn't had food for a long time. This seemed to help clear her head a bit, too, and she suddenly had a lot of questions. "So, how did you know who I was? How did you know where to find me? Who are you guys anyway?"

Ty answered her questions with one of his own. "I promise we'll tell you all that, Dawna, if you tell your side of the story to us first."

She took a deep breath. "I'm from a really small town. Sierraville has about 350 people and I guess I just felt stuck there. I had dreams of being a model, you know? My parents weren't able to help me with that. It wasn't their fault; they are great parents. I can't believe what I've put them through!" At this she stopped and buried her face in her hands again. Sammy and Tiff patted her gently on the back.

"Anyway," she continued when she had composed herself, "I decided to take matters into my own hands and ran away. I walked up to the highway and hitched rides to Sacramento. My plan was to get to San Francisco or maybe LA and try to break into the modeling business. The problem is that once I got to Sacramento, I was scared and hungry and didn't know where to go. That's where I met Chad. At least, that's what I thought his name was. I was hanging out at the bus terminal in Sacramento, trying to bum enough money to get to San Francisco, when this guy came up to me offering to make me a star. I was just scared and lonely, ya know? He took me out to eat, and let me tell you I was starved! He was handsome and very persuasive.

He offered what I'd always wanted, but it didn't turn out to be what I had hoped."

Tiff remembered her meeting with Chad at the truck stop. Would she have fallen for his charms if she hadn't been up there looking for Dawna? She had a hard time imagining it, but then, she'd never been hungry or desperate. Her life back home was looking much better.

"What happened next?" asked Tiff to keep Dawna talking.

"Well, Chad – Johnny, that is – told me he had a gig for me. He said I had to prove myself before he'd be willing to let me model for real. He took me to meet Gary, the red-bearded guy and the two other girls. That's when I knew something wasn't right. I could see it in their eyes. The girls – I don't even know their names – they looked drugged. They never let us talk to each other, but then he drove us to that truck area tonight and…" she started to cry again. "They sold me to that trucker for sex! I just couldn't believe it. I was so scared. Then he threw me out of the truck and there you were!"

Tiff was tracking with Dawna's story until it seemed to stop making sense. Had she really said tonight was the first night she'd been in a truck?

"Wait a minute?" said Ty, confusion in his voice. "Are you saying that tonight was the first time that Gary tried to sell you to the truck drivers?"

"Yes," said Dawna between sobs.

"How long have you been with him?"

"Johnny picked me up at the bus station yesterday. They have this fleabag apartment in Sacramento. He let me sleep on the couch last night. When I slept most of the day, I thought I was just tired, but maybe they drugged me, too. Tonight, Gary came with the other girls and picked us up. Gary told Johnny to drive and where to pull over. We had to wait in the van in a dark parking lot while Johnny went to get some hamburgers. The burgers were small and Gary kept telling us to hurry up and eat while Johnny was driving us to that rest stop."

"Wait, wait," said Ty, sounding as confused as Tiff felt. "When exactly did you run away from home?"

"Well," she said, thinking, "I left Monday. I remember because I pretended to walk down the lane to catch the bus for summer school."

"You left home *this* Monday?" asked Lando, mystified.

"Yes," said Dawna. "I planned my get-away on the weekend and acted as if nothing had changed. Then I left for school on Monday. Geeze, it feels like a lifetime ago, and it's been what, three or four days? What day is today?"

"Officially, since its three-thirty A.M., it's Thursday," informed Tiff.

"I just don't get it," said Ty, shaking his head. He was trying to comprehend how this girl they'd been planning to find for three weeks left home only a few days ago. He pulled the car over and turned to look at Dawna. "So you're telling me that you ran away Monday and tonight was the first time you were in a truck."

"That's right," said Dawna.

Ty turned back to the front, and tilted his head to the side, thinking.

Everyone sat waiting. Tiff was beginning to comprehend. The information they were given about Dawna was given to implement her rescue before anything bad happened to her. *Well, being kidnapped is bad enough,* realized Tiff, *but it could have been so much worse.* She glanced at Ty and saw him wipe his eyes. She was shocked speechless.

"What don't you get? Did I say something wrong? Are you going to tell me your story now? Did my parents send you after me or something?" asked Dawna.

Tiff took a breath. "Well, it's kind of a long story."

"And you might not believe it," added Sammy.

"I guess we should just start at the beginning," said Lando.

Ty pulled back onto the road and they began to talk, explaining everything that led them to her. After they'd finished, the car was silent for a long time. Dawna drifted into sleep while Tiff sat mulling over the revelation. They woke Dawna when they got close to Sierraville.

"The thing I don't get is why and how we all started getting this information so long before it happened?" said Ty.

"Yeah, that's pretty wild," Dawna admitted. "I'd say you were the answer to my prayers. But those prayers hadn't even been prayed yet."

"Dawna, what happens when we get to your house?" asked Tiff.

"I guess I'll go in and tell my folks I'm home."

"Will you tell them everything that happened?" asked Sammy.

"I don't know. They'll be so hurt. What should I do? I'm so embarrassed."

Sammy had an answer. "Dawna, listen to me. You need to be completely honest with your parents. You have to tell them *everything* and you'll probably need to make a police report right away. It will be really hard, but you have to be super brave. It's important these guys get put away for good and aren't allowed to hurt any more girls. Your information will help convict them."

Tiff was amazed by Sammy's statement. The other day – was it really only yesterday – she'd seemed unsure about whether telling about the abuse had been the right decision. Now she was encouraging Dawna to do just that. *Wow, Sammy has changed so much.*

"Are you sure I have to tell them?" asked Dawna weakly.

"Dawna, something similar happened to me and I had to tell. My telling saved my little sister from going through what I went through. Do you have a sister?"

"I do. Emily, she's 14, only two years younger than me. I have two little brothers, too."

"Dawna, I only wish I'd told sooner. Promise me you will tell."

Dawna stared at Sammy in the dark, considering what she would do. Nodding, she asked. "What do I say about you guys?"

"Uh, we'd appreciate it if you didn't bring us up at all," said Ty.

"Well, how am I supposed to have gotten home?"

"Say you hitched a ride with some kids, but you didn't get their names. You were too upset," suggested Ty. "We'd rather not be pulled into this. You see, no one knows about our, uh, story, no one but you."

"Okay, but how can I ever thank you? You saved my life!"

"No thanks needed. Maybe my dreams will stop now and I'll get a good night's sleep for a change. That will be enough for me. Just stay safe, okay?"

"I will," she promised. She stretched up to look out the window and pointed to the left. "My house is really close now. I never thought I'd be so excited to be home!" She gave Ty directions as he drove. Finally, she pointed down a long lane to a white house surrounded by trees. "That's my house down there."

"Mind if we drop you off here?" asked Ty.

"No, that's probably best," she agreed. They all filed out of the car and gave Dawna hugs.

Sammy said, "I've changed my mind. I need to go in with her."

"What?" asked Ty. "Sammy, we don't want to get any more involved than we are, and we need to get home!"

"No," said Lando, "let her go. It'll be okay."

They could not see Ty roll his eyes in the dark, but they knew he wasn't happy. Sammy and Dawna headed up the driveway toward the dark house. Tiff couldn't see what happened next, but suddenly lights came on in the house and there was a lot of loud shouting.

CHAPTER TWENTY-THREE
HOMECOMINGS

AFTER OPENING THE DOOR WITH A KEY taken from under the welcome mat, Dawna and Sammy entered the small, but cozy home. Dawna tried to enter as quietly as possible, but her family must have been on high alert because soon lights came on all over the house. The living room suddenly felt full as her mother, father, sister and brothers entered the room.

"Dawna Jean, where have you been!" wailed her distraught mother before bursting into tears and throwing her arms around her daughter. They both started sobbing. Her father wrapped both of them in his arms and let his tears fall into their hair. A gawky teenage girl stood nearby, arms folded tightly against her chest. Two smaller boys hovered around the living room, unable or unsure of what to do with themselves. Sammy stood near the door equally unsure why she was there.

When the melée of tears had slowed, a barrage of questions started flooding the room from every person: "Where have you been? Are you okay? Why did you leave? How could you do that to us?" One question stopped everyone in their tracks: "How did you escape?" This question came from Dawna's fourteen-year-old sister, Emily.

"What?" asked Dawna. "How did you know?"

"I had a dream," said Emily, looking angry. "And that girl," she said pointing directly at Sammy, "helped you escape." Dawna's parents seemed to see Sammy for the first time. They looked at her in wonder.

"Hi," Sammy said into the silence. "I just wanted to make sure Dawna got home safely."

Dawna's father released his hug and grabbed Dawna's shoulders. "Then Emily's dream was right? Someone had taken you? And, this girl," he nodded to Sammy, "helped you escape?"

Dawna was quiet, not sure how to answer these questions.

Sammy jumped in, "Dawna has been through a lot, but she is safe now and will need your support. She'll want to make a police report."

"But who are you?" asked Dawna's mother. "How did you find our Dawna?"

"Well, I'd guess you'd say it was divine intervention. Unfortunately, I need to get home myself. I just wanted to make sure Dawna was okay here."

"Of course she's okay here," said her mother sharply. "She's home!"

Sammy nodded her yes and turned to leave. Dawna tried to move toward her, but her parents held onto her. Sammy gave Dawna a smile, who grinned back, eyes brimming with gratitude.

Before Sammy could pull the door closed behind her, it was opened by Dawna's sister, Emily, who poked her head out of the opening. "Hey," she said in a small voice, "thank you." She looked like she wanted to say more but ran out of words. Sammy nodded.

She joined her friends in the car, and they headed towards home as she filled them in on the encounter inside the house.

"Another dreamer," said Ty, shaking his head. "What is happening here?"

No one really had an answer for him. They were overwhelmed with all they had witnessed, and as their adrenalin began to ebb, their physical exhaustion became evident. They tried different tricks to help Ty stay awake as he drove. They rolled down the windows, blasted music and even played twenty questions. But as they approached Reno, their fatigue was replaced with fear about what would happen when they got home.

"No way I'm getting up for school tomorrow, or today, that is," said Tiff.

"Mr. Monahan said we could miss two days and none of us have missed any," added Lando.

"I think we all deserve some sleep," agreed Ty.

"If we survive getting in the door unnoticed," said Tiff. "I will be grounded for the rest of my life if they catch me sneaking in!"

Fortunately, no one seemed to notice the early morning arrival of either of the girls as they tiptoed toward their own beds. Lando and Ty weren't so lucky. Lando arrived home to find his Grandmother sitting on the couch in the living room. He came in and sat down next to her, not sure what to say. "*Buenos días, Abuela* ," he began, tentatively wishing his grandmother a good morning.

"Orlando," his grandmother said in Spanish, "I'm so glad you are home. I had the most interesting dream about you."

"Really *Abuela*? What was it?"

"I dreamed that you were a champion for the cause of those who could not help themselves. Especially, you were championing the cause of women who were being threatened."

"Wow, *Abuela* that is a good dream. I would very much like to be that kind of person."

His grandmother looked at him for a long time. "I believe you will," she said with great certainty. "Perhaps you already are. Now, go to bed my love."

Lando walked away in wonder at the response from his grandmother. It seemed he'd escaped whatever wrath she would normally have given him, and all because of a dream.

It's odd about dreams, he thought, as he quickly drifted into a deep and dreamless sleep.

TY GOT TO HIS HOUSE LATEST. It was almost six after he dropped everyone else off. He came in the back door and was next to the kitchen when his mother, coming around the corner, turned on the light. She jumped, startled to see him.

"Tyrell, you scared me to death! What are you doing up so early?"

Ty stood still like a deer caught in headlights. It dawned on him slowly that his mother thought he was up early instead of getting home late. "Couldn't sleep," he said, trying to sound groggy. "I don't feel so good."

"Oh," she said, stretching up high to feel his forehead and searching his face. "Young man, you get right back in bed; you look awful! And don't you even think about going to school today."

"Uh, okay Mama," he said, "if you say so." He shuffled off to bed, thanking his lucky stars.

CHAPTER TWENTY-FOUR
NEW BEGINNINGS

TY SAT ON THE COLD METAL STAIRS of the portable early before class on Monday. He wanted to catch Mr. Monahan entering the class, before the other students arrived. He was still trying to formulate an explanation for his group's absence when he heard the sound of a longboard coming around the portable's front end.

"Hey, Ty," Mr. Monahan said as he leapt off the board and flipped it up into his hand. "What brings you out so early this fine morning?"

"Hey, Mr. Monahan. I wanted to apologize for the blue group's absence yesterday."

"I was wondering about that. You guys all catch the same flu bug or something?" He walked up the stairs that Ty was standing on and unlocked the portable door. Ty followed him into the small classroom.

"Well, not exactly, but we helped a – a friend, and it took longer than we'd expected. I'm really sorry."

"You missed the last group presentation. Maybe you should apologize to the yellow group. They did a great job on their report."

"That's a good idea. I'm really sorry." Ty knew it was inadequate but couldn't think of what else to say.

"Ty, there's something I'd like to ask you about the blue group. It's just you all seem to get along so well and so quickly. I mean, you're from different schools. You're different ages and you're different ethnicities. What is it that's bonded you together?"

Ty stood quietly, thinking, and finally he answered, "I don't really know. I guess we have more in common than one would think." His expression, previously serious, now lit up like the sun.

"Ty, I'm bummed you guys skipped out on class Thursday. But honestly, if any group were to do it, yours was the one that could best afford to. Yet somehow I thought yours was also the most unlikely. I guess you really were helping a friend?"

"Yes, we were."

Mr. Monahan stood waiting for a further explanation, but Ty was silent.

"Then I suppose if you don't miss this last week of school, we're cool. Maybe the yellow group will let you make copies of their reports to read if you ask them nicely." He smiled.

"Thanks!" Ty went outside to wait for his friends.

THEY SAT ON THE GRASS IN THE WARM July sunlight. Each blue group member shared in amazement about how they'd gotten back into their houses without getting in trouble.

"Thanks for getting the journaling assignment to us, Tiff," said Sammy.

"No prob, I'm friends with Chandra on Facebook, so I got it from her. Who wants to go first?"

"How 'bout the usual?" suggested Sammy. "You start us off, Tiff."

"Okay," agreed Tiff, remembering how painful the idea of going first had been only three weeks ago. *A lifetime ago,* she thought. Picking up her worn blue binder, she flipped toward the back to read. "What have I learned so far from being in this class/group? I'd have to say I learned more from being in this English class than I'd ever expected. Not just about English although you are a terrific teacher Mr. Monahan–"

"Kiss-up," said Sammy.

"Hey," countered Tiff smiling, "I'm just saying." She continued to read: "I learned not to look on the outside of people." Glancing up from her reading, she smiled at Sammy, "but, to wait patiently for glimpses of their heart. It's worth the wait."

Sammy smiled at her and gave her a thumb's up.

"And I learned that people who have experienced hurt, whether directly or indirectly," she looked over at Lando, "can make the bravest advocates for others who have been hurt." He smiled at her shyly.

"I also learned that God doesn't really care about whether or not we believe in him." She looked pointedly at Ty who tilted his head at her, lips pursed skeptically. "Because, if He believes in you – well then that's enough to change the world."

She closed her binder with a slap.

"I'm next," said Ty, opening his binder. "I think the most important thing I learned in this class was to trust other people. I used to think I could figure out everything on my own, but I've learned that alone we can only do so much, but together we can make a big difference. I learned to listen and not to react so much although I'm still working on that one." He glanced up and smiled at his friends, who nodded in agreement. "I learned I don't have all the answers. I've learned not everything that happens in life makes sense logically or scientifically. And although I don't like that fact, it seems to be true." He shut the binder and grinned.

"My turn," said Lando, lifting his binder. "I learned a lot from this class. I learned my family history is not something to run from but something that will make me a stronger person. And, I learned I have skills!" He looked up, smiling at his friends, who grinned back. "I learned that I can study and that I'm good at public speaking. I'm brave and I'm strong. These are all qualities I got from my mom and my grandmother. I learned I have strong opinions about things, and I can use my voice and skills to help those who are in trouble. Mostly, I learned that life is way more interesting with friends in it." He closed his binder, smiling.

"It's all you, Sammy," said Tiff.

Sammy opened the battered blue binder that had the picture of the knight on the front. "I wrote a poem," she said, taking a deep breath. "It's called 'Opening the Cage.'"

She gave her friends a wobbly smile and began to read.

Opening the Cage

Open, open wide the cage door and let the small bird fly.

No longer to be kept inside,wings clipped in fear and pain.

Who can open the door to free the trapped bird?

Only those who care enough to take the risk of love.

Only those willing to face danger, heartache and rejection.

Only those who hear the voice and see the frightened eyes,

and let their hearts be moved,

not just to compassion, but

To action.

Where are those who can open the cage?

They are here, all around you, open your scared eyes and see.

Then, join the fight to save others trapped by fear.

You know how to hear their small voices,

You can see their frightened eyes,

Then your pain will begin, to not just heal, but to offer healing.

Not to fade, but to make sense.

Not to "get over" but to "move beyond."

Then your name will change

From frightened bird,

to loved bird,

to freer of birds.

ACKNOWLEDGMENTS

I NOW UNDERSTAND IT TAKES A VILLAGE to write a book! My first shoutout goes to my family: David the husband of my youth, thank you for believing in my dream. Sarah, my Boo, you are the cheerleader that helped me at every step from first edit to last, and my incredible Website. Thank you for your love and support. Micah boy, thank you for asking me, from places far and near, "How is your writing, Mom?" and saying, "Don't give up!"

To Judith Harlan, my writing guru, and my friends at Luckybatbooks.com, I hope ours will be a long and happy friendship. Your belief in this project was a great encouragement!

Thank you to those who helped check my cultural competence. If there are mistakes, they are mine alone. Thank you: Jessica Osborne, Phil Bowling-Dyer and Tiera Morton for checks on Tyrell's family life. Thanks to Theresa Cho, Hanju Lee and Brian Son for help on Tiffany's family life. Thanks for Cecilia Khan and for help on Orlando's family life.

Someone said writing a book is like picking out a stone to sculpt; the rest is editing. This has been true for me. Thanks to all my friends from the Unnamed Writer's Group in Reno who critiqued and edited this book: Peggy Rew, Mat Bayan, Barbara Jean, Derryl Baker and

Kay Brooks you guys are awesome! Thanks to Susi Jensen, can't wait to read yours!

To our adoptees, Chris and Natalie Heifner, she for being a first reader and he for designing my wonderful cover and trailer! You two rock!

To all my friends and extended family, such love. You brighten my days. I can't thank you all by name but the Monday Girls and Wednesday Girls deserve a special shout-out for all your support. To my IVCF colleges, your love carries me. Vicky – road trip?

Thanks Mom, Skye and Carl for being first readers. And thanks Dad for instilling in me a love of reading and modeling a love of writing. I know you're happy for me.

To Barbara Ernst, my spiritual director, and all my friends at Mercy Center in Auburn, thank you for a great and safe place to let me write and the encouragement to do so.

I'd also like to thank two authors who encouraged me never to give up but to keep writing: Anne Lamott and Jennifer Lauck. The world is a better place because you're in it.

To God who gives good gifts to all, thank you for this one.

Dear Reader,

This book covers some difficult topics. You might relate to being in a cage. Please let me know if you are struggling with things and want to talk. Find me at http://www.Jacciturner.com

If you are struggling with cutting, depression or self-injury find help at: To Write Love on Her Arms, http://www.twloha.com/vision/

If you have been sexually abused, find help at RAINN, http://www.rainn.org/

To learn more about how to stop the sex-trafficking of children, go to, Not for Sale at, http://www.notforsalecampaign.org/

Ten percent of the profits of this book will go towards building safe houses for rescued trafficked children through the work of: http://www.couragetobeyou.org/